DAMSEL IN DISTRESS

Gus was fast asleep, his wool stocking cap pulled tightly down over his ears, dark pursuers and ladies in distress about the furthest thing in the world from his mind. When a sudden hammering at the lighthouse door broke in upon his slumbers, he popped bolt upright in confusion.

"Why, what's going on? What's the commotion?" he cried, at the same time trying to untangle himself from his blanket in the dark.

The only answer was more pounding. Fumbling to light a candle, Gus heaved himself to his feet, clad only in his wool cap, baggy trousers held up by string and an old shirt flapping open to the waist. He unlatched the door—and was almost knocked down by the person who rushed in, sweeping Gus halfway across the room before a veritable storm of rustling skirts and wind-swirled cloak. Not only was the intruder a woman, it was a young one, beautiful and apparently terrified.

"I need sanctuary!" she blurted out in a voice throaty and vulnerable.

Also available in the Road to Avonlea Series from Bantam Skylark books

A Dark and Stormy Night

Storybook written by

Gail Hamilton

Based on the Sullivan Films Production
written by Gail Hamilton
adapted from the novels of

Lucy Maud Montgomery

Based on the Sullivan Films Production produced by Sullivan Films Inc.
in association with CBC and the Disney Channel with the participation
of Telefilm Canada adapted from Lucy Maud Montgomery's novels.

Teleplay written by Gail Hamilton
Copyright © 1991 by Sullivan Films Distribution, Inc.

This edition contains the complete text
of the original edition.
NOT ONE WORD HAS BEEN OMITTED.

RL 6, 008–012

A DARK AND STORMY NIGHT
A Bantam Skylark Book / published by arrangement with
HarperCollins Publishers Ltd.

PUBLISHING HISTORY
HarperCollins edition published 1994
Bantam edition / November 1994

ISBN 0-553-48124-X

PRINTED IN THE UNITED STATES OF AMERICA
OPM 0 9 8 7 6 5 4 3 2 1

Chapter One

"'At midnight,'" read Sara Stanley, by the light of the fire leaping in the grate, "'the wicked Count left the ruined castle again, charging through the darkness, his eyes glittering like those of a demon, his soul black and malevolent, stricken by jealousy, death his only objective....'"

Sara's voice rose and fell in thrilling crescendos, holding her listeners spellbound as she read aloud from the shockingly lurid magazine serial. Sara and her audience, consisting of her three King cousins, sat all alone in the King family farmhouse, which creaked with mysterious noises and groaned in the wind at the scariest parts of the story. What's more, the night outside was so black and wild, the children could imagine that a wicked count *might* be galloping abroad, even through the fields of peaceful, rural Avonlea.

Cecily King, Sara's youngest cousin, sat with her arms around Digger, the family dog, tightly clutching his reassuring, furry warmth. Felicity, the eldest, was made of sterner stuff. She sat at the table calmly stitching rhinestones onto the bodice of a dress. Only the brightness of her eyes and the periodic heave of her bosom betrayed how intently she was listening. At fourteen, two years older than Sara, Felicity had been left temporarily in charge of the household. She could not afford to give the impression that she feared the ravages of unhinged aristocrats, no matter how many demons glittered in their eyes. Felix, the middle cousin and the only boy present, felt it his masculine duty to scoff at the Count's carryings-on.

"All this because some girl won't pledge her troth — whatever that is," Felix grumbled in a disgusted manner, reaching towards the sadly depleted cookie plate.

"She won't marry him and his heart has turned to stone," Felicity explained rather shortly to her unromantic brother. "Not that *you'd* know anything about passion!"

At eleven, Felix was interested only in the chase scenes and the murders, the gorier the better. Felicity, on the other hand, was blossoming into a young woman. The first tender fancies of adulthood swirled about in her soul. She felt in a position to appreciate all the finer points of lovestruck souls and hearts shattered into madness by cruelly broken pledges.

"A man possessed by a twisted passion," Sara confirmed from the depths of her armchair, not taking her eyes from the story. The magazine was neatly tucked inside a large, respectable copy of *Aesop's Fables*, which was what the children were really supposed to be reading. Magazine serials were severely looked down upon by the adult Kings, especially by the children's formidable Aunt Hetty, who not only taught school in Avonlea but considered herself the local arbiter of all things tasteful and refined.

"He has a castle with a moat, a thousand servants to bring him whatever he wants," Felix protested doggedly about the Count. "I don't see why he's always riding around in the dark killing people."

Twisted passion obviously meant little to Felix, who thought the Count spoiled and petulant. If a fellow were fortunate enough to have his stomach always full and no chores to do, there was certainly no need to go rampaging about the countryside murdering folks in the dark!

Sara glanced up warningly, not used to unappreciative comments from her audience. Her theatrical powers were something of a legend in Avonlea. She had, after all, once moved an entire crowded Town Hall to tears with her recitation of "The Poor Little Match Girl," frozen to death in the snow. Now, on top of Felix's skepticism, Cecily seemed to be falling asleep.

"'The stench of death—'" she began to read.

"Unrequited love has driven him mad, is all," Felicity cut in, determined to squelch Felix once and for all.

"Oh, phooey on all that," Felix shot back. He wished he had just one of those thousand servants to split all the wood he'd had to pile up that day.

"If you want me to stop reading, I will," Sara said, exasperated. "I'm only supposed to be staying with you while your parents are away so Felicity can teach me something about running a household."

Sara actually lived down the lane at Rose Cottage with her Aunt Hetty. After Sara's parents had died, she had moved from Montreal to live with her King relatives permanently. She loved the country and she loved Avonlea, but she sometimes felt herself far more cosmopolitan than her cousins could ever be. On the other hand, unlike Felicity, Sara had grown up with servants and had arrived in Avonlea without the faintest idea how to make herself useful around a house or barn. The Kings were working to remedy that situation as quickly as they could.

"For your information, Sara Stanley, reading aloud to the children is a very important part of running the household," Felicity informed her loftily.

Felicity would never admit that she herself was dying to find out what calamities the Count's twisted passion would lead to. With a small, knowing quirk of her lips, Sara went back to the magazine.

"'When he grimaced,'" she continued, taking up the description of one of love's more extreme casualties, "'his teeth flashed like the razor-sharp canines of half-starved dogs. The peasants huddled by their hearths, their doors locked against the stormy dark, knowing Lord Doom had once again laid claim to the night.'"

Cecily slept on, mercifully oblivious to such nightmare-inducing fare. Felix and Felicity, despite the comments bubbling inside them, actually bit their lips to keep from interrupting Sara again and having her stop the story.

It took only a moment before both listeners were completely swept up, for when Sara read, she flung herself into it, heart and soul. Her breathless, hypnotic words brought the tale of Lord Doom vividly to life in the imaginations of her cousins. The windows rattling in their frames might have been Lord Doom demanding entry. The lashing of a tree branch against the kitchen wall might have been the lashing of his riding crop, and both Felix and Felicity shivered involuntarily with delicious terror. Felicity stopped sewing mid-stitch as the Count lurched towards his next victim. Felix forgot to breathe. And placid Digger, the least likely to care about Lord Doom, suddenly leapt to his feet, threw back his head and howled.

Felix and Felicity jumped clean out of their chairs. Sara dropped the magazine to the floor and Cecily reeled abruptly awake as Digger sprang from her embrace. Digger was now barking madly, leaping at the door to get out. In fact, he was acting as though Lord Doom might be out there, menacing the barn. Since Digger was the farm watchdog, Felix opened the door to see what Digger was barking about. Immediately, Digger thrust himself through the opening and vanished, still barking, into the gloom.

"Digger! Come back, boy!" Felicity shouted,

running to the door herself. The dog wasn't supposed to be out at night.

"You scared him," Felix muttered to Sara.

"I didn't even know he was listening!" Sara was secretly hoping that Digger wasn't going to fall victim to some crazed blueblood out on a tear.

Felix began to pull on his boots and his coat.

"Where do you think you're going?" Felicity demanded. In the absence of her parents, she was responsible for the rest of the children.

"I"m going to get Digger, of course."

"I forbid it." Felicity's glower indicated that he wasn't about to have Felix running around by himself in the wintry night.

"When the Hodgins let their dog out at night, it was mistaken for a wolf by Mr. Armstrong," Felix countered worriedly.

Mr. Armstrong was a less than friendly neighbor quite fanatical about guarding his sheep. Anything that looked faintly like a wolf faced the business end of Mr. Armstrong's shotgun.

"That's true, Felicity," Sara put in, suddenly anxious about Digger too.

To clinch the matter, Cecily began wailing, terrified that she'd never see her beloved dog again. Assaulted from all sides, Felicity put her hands on her hips.

"It's all your fault, Sara Stanley," she exclaimed, as though Digger had understood every word of the story.

"I didn't want to read it anyway," Sara protested. "I wanted to read *Aesop's Fables*!"

This was not strictly true, but Sara felt bound to pay lip service to the principles of good taste. She loved a good, hair-raising melodrama just as much as the next person.

Felicity made a swift decision.

"Fine, then. We'll all go. Cecily, you stay here in case Digger comes back."

Chapter Two

Digger might not have understood what Sara had been reading, but he had excellent hearing nonetheless. He darted from the house and made straight across the fields towards the nearby cliffs, which dropped precipitously to the sea rolling in below. The cliffs, at that time of night, were not at all inviting. The path along their edge was scoured by a frigid wind that whipped at the waves and drove clouds before it across the face of a remote, icy moon. The ground all around was frosty, barren and filled with pitfalls for anyone foolish enough to venture into them by night.

Nevertheless, someone, or something, was venturing out that night. Digger had been attracted by a sound — the distant, staccato thunder of hoofbeats cutting through the freezing air. A rider suddenly burst into view, hurtling through the night at a full gallop, head bent and a dark cloak billowing out from his shoulders.

He approached so quickly that great clods of mud flew up from the horse's pounding hooves. The horse was huge and black, blacker than the very midnight it galloped through, its ebony mane streaming backward in the wind and snorts of steaming breath issuing from its nostrils. The rider whipped it mercilessly for yet more speed, his whip slashing down as he searched the ground before him and scanned the path as far ahead as his eyes could see.

He had to be a stranger, for no quiet inhabitant of Avonlea could have sat so tall and so threateningly in the saddle. No inhabitant of Avonlea could have spurred the horse so ruthlessly, this way and that, as though in search of some unfortunate quarry escaping before him. Lord Doom himself could not have looked more startling as he hunted down his victims through the terrified countryside.

And the quarry was real, though even Digger missed it in his rush to make for the rider. A silhouette sped along the cliff's edge, a figure on foot, running desperately, diving into the shadows when it could. Human quarry, exactly the same as that scurrying about in the corners of Lord Doom's vast estates.

What's more, the silhouette belonged to a woman, hooded and cloaked and stumbling as she ran. Though seemingly close to the end of her strength, she forced herself on, her breath coming fast, visible on the chilly air. Then the breaths stopped altogether as the sound of hoofbeats finally reached her. Petrified, she peered behind her just as the dark rider crested a knoll, showing himself for a moment against the moon-paled sky.

A gasp tore from the woman's throat. She looked about her frantically, catching sight of the only structure visible in that desolate landscape, the old lighthouse that clung to the very edge of the steep red cliffs. Gathering her cloak around her, she began to run towards it. She was in such a hurry to escape the horseman that she didn't dare pause, even when one of her shoes flew off and lay behind her, its elegant buckle winking in the mud.

The lighthouse, for all its abandoned look, did have an inhabitant. Young Gus Pike lived there.

Not seventeen, Gus had arrived in Avonlea fresh off a fishing boat, almost penniless and living by his wits. Rough and illiterate, he ended up working in the fish cannery and seemed destined for life as a drifter. Yet Gus turned out to be different from his coarse fellows at the cannery. Under his unpolished exterior, Gus had the heart of a gentleman, an intelligent mind and a thirst to better himself.

Luckily for him, he had been scooped up in one of Hetty King's periodic campaigns to expand enrollment in the Avonlea school. Gus had braved the jeers of his fellows, working nights in the cannery so that he could go to school by day. Bravely, he sat cheek by jowl with children years younger than himself as he learned to read and write and not smoke his pipe in school.

Gus always had to scratch to support himself. Since leaving the cannery, he had been living off a series of odd jobs, each a little better than the last, as he continued his education. He saved himself the cost of rent by moving into the cramped lighthouse after fierce Captain Crane, who had previously occupied it, had decided to go back to sea.

At the very moment when Digger was bounding across the fields, Gus was fast asleep, his wool stocking cap pulled tightly down over his ears, dark pursuers and ladies in distress about the furthest thing in the world from his mind. When a sudden hammering at the lighthouse door broke in upon his slumber, he sat bolt upright in confusion.

"Why, what's going on? What's the commotion?" he cried, at the same time trying to untangle himself from his blanket.

The only answer was more pounding. Fumbling to light a lamp, Gus heaved himself to his feet, clad only in his wool cap, baggy trousers held up by string and an old shirt flapping open to the waist. He unlatched the door—and was almost knocked down by the person who rushed in, sweeping Gus halfway across the room before a veritable storm of rustling skirts and wind-swirled cloak. Not only was the intruder a woman, she was a young one, beautiful and apparently terrified.

"I need sanctuary!" she blurted out in a voice throaty and vulnerable.

Dumfounded, Gus simply stood, staring. "What's this?" he demanded weakly.

The woman turned in a panic, her cloud of glossy hair tumbling in charming tendrils from its knot.

"May I bar your door, sir?" she begged.

Since no one ever barred a door in the Avonlea vicinity, Gus blinked even harder.

"Well, sure ma'am," he stammered. "But I don't usually."

Swiftly, the mysterious intruder flung the rusty bolt across the door while Gus bestirred himself to light the lamp. In the burst of light, Gus suddenly became aware of his own state of undress, most unseemly in the presence of a lady. He crossed his arms over his chest in a vain attempt to maintain some modesty, as his visitor turned back to him.

Her eyes widened when she saw how young he really was and how astounded by her presence. In the yellow lamplight, the contrast between them was thrown into high relief. Though young herself, the visitor was a woman in her twenties, clad in rich silks and in full command of her own femininity. And she took full advantage of that femininity by flinging one hand to her bosom.

"Oh, please hide me, I'm in grave danger and there isn't much time."

Unable to move a muscle, Gus continued to gape. The lady saw that more direct action was necessary if she were to have a hiding place before the hour was out. She swayed forward and promptly swooned straight into Gus's arms.

In the barest nick of time, Gus caught her, and he was immediately enveloped in a cloud of intoxicating perfume. Stunned, he had absolutely no idea what to do with this beautiful armful.

Outside, not so very far down the track, the galloping rider had pulled his horse up short while he scanned the half-frozen earth around him for clues. As he did so, a tattered cloud slid away from the moon, revealing a man forbidding enough to be an actual relative of Lord Doom. Even taller than he had looked from a distance, he sat ramrod straight in the saddle, his every motion driven, it seemed, by some fearful determination that could only end in the achievement of his purpose. His expression was locked into ominous lines, and a glitter of triumph leaped into his eye as he suddenly spotted the woman's shoe mired in the mud.

Dismounting, he pounced upon it, gripping it in his fist as he looked around him for the direction in which his quarry might have fled. Just as the woman had, he spied the lighthouse looming up against the moon-touched horizon.

With a grunt of cold satisfaction, he was just turning back to his horse when Digger loped out of the night, determined to investigate the interloper. Though the dog would have been satisfied with a friendly sniff, he suddenly found a hard kick aimed in his direction.

"Get out of here you ... mangy critter."

Digger, for all his easygoing nature, was not

one to be threatened on his own territory. After all, he had a farm and children to protect. He stood his ground and growled back.

The man swung back up into his saddle, clearly meaning to leave Digger behind in the dust. Digger was having none of this. He lunged forward, clamping his teeth onto the edge of the man's long, trailing cloak. Digger's weight nearly unseated the rider as he struggled to keep his balance atop his rearing mount.

Perhaps the horse really did mistake Digger for a wolf, for it began to bolt. With a curse, the man ripped the cloak from Digger's grip and went careening off towards the lighthouse. Digger was only prevented from hot pursuit by the calls in the distance of Sara and her cousins, reaching him between the gusts of wind.

Inside the lighthouse, Gus hurriedly thrust the unconscious female into the only possible hiding place, a crawl space that lay unexpectedly behind one of the sections of old wall. He was just dragging a heavy trunk across the opening when his door was kicked open, as though the rusty bolt had not been there at all. Gus found his home invaded a second time, this time by a glowering stranger clutching a lady's shoe in his fist.

"Hey!" Gus yelped as an icy blast from outside nearly knocked him backward.

The stranger thrust Gus aside as though he were a cobweb and looked about the interior, seeing nothing but bits of rough furniture, Gus's few precious books and some old fishing tackle. Gus recovered his balance and began to bristle.

"Who said you could just rampage a fella's door and walk in?" he shouted, outraged. Humble as the place was, it was still his home, and therefore his castle.

The lamplight revealed a man who was very handsome in a hard, frightening sort of way, clad in dashing, well-cut clothes and with a shock of black, wind-tangled hair sweeping across his forehead. Ignoring Gus, he proceeded to search the room, flinging Gus's meager belongings out of his path, turning over chairs and tables with reckless force. Only when the search proved fruitless did the stranger acknowledge Gus. He did it by suddenly grabbing Gus by his open shirt and shaking him sharply.

"Where is she, or do I have to snap you in two?"

This was certainly no way for a visitor to act. Stubbornly, Gus said nothing, not even when lifted clear off the ground and then flung down again in disgust. The stranger tore up the room a second time, heaving items about even more fiercely than before. When Gus's battered tin soup pot clanged into a corner and not so much as a trace of any female was revealed, the man finally stopped, gritting his teeth in frustration.

"You can't hide from me forever, Amanda Stone!" he shouted out, shaking his fist at the empty air, as if the woman addressed might be hovering invisibly, making fun of him.

He seemed about to give up when he spotted the large trunk blocking the crawl space. As the man advanced upon it, Gus valiantly sprang forward.

"Hey! This is my place—"

"Don't trifle with me, boy!"

The stranger tossed Gus aside with one hand and, with the other, jerked impatiently at the lid of the trunk. The lid came open with a squeal—only to reveal an interior full to the brim with lead fishing weights. Before the rude brute got ideas about moving it away from the wall, Gus staggered to his feet and made another run at his opponent. No lady deserved to fall into the hands of a ruffian like this!

Gus barely covered two steps before the man swung round, striking the boy on the side of the head with one of the lead weights. The sheer force of the blow sent Gus sprawling into a heap all the way against the far wall, his wool cap knocked off in the skirmish.

Whatever else this terrible man intended to do was prevented by the appearance of Digger in the open doorway. Digger's temper had been sorely tried by the stranger's previous behavior. And what's more, the nasty fellow was now storming about the home of Digger's good friend, Gus Pike.

Just in case the invader had any thoughts about trying a second kick, Digger began to growl. He growled fiercely enough to make the stranger realize he was cornered in a small room by a large dog that he had very recently mistreated. He eyed Digger warily, then caught the sounds of the children calling in the darkness. In a frustrated rage, he turned to the room behind him.

"I'll never give up," he shouted at the upended furniture. " I'll chase you to the ends of the earth if I must."

With that, the man flung down the shoe he was holding and stamped towards the door. Feeling he had gained the upper hand, Digger prudently backed up enough to allow the interloper out into the night. When the room was clear, Digger trotted over to where Gus lay in the dust and began licking the boy's face vigorously.

With a grunt, Gus pushed the dog away and struggled to sit up, rubbing the side of his head where the weight had hit him. When he realized the room was empty, he got all the way to his feet and made his way woozily to the window to see what had become of his attacker. All that could be heard were hoofbeats receding into the night.

With a huge sigh of relief, Gus at once hurried over to the trunk and placed his back against the wall. Using all his strength, he managed to move it far enough out into the room to reveal the woman he had hidden. She had made a miraculous recovery from her swoon and had curled up quite comfortably in the cramped, dark space.

Chapter Three

Some distance away, Sara, Felicity and Felix were tramping through the cold in search of Digger. A night like this would have been scary enough, but with the grisly exploits of Lord Doom fresh in their minds, each youngster was becoming more and more terrified as they blundered along, holding onto each other, by the light of the eerie white moon.

Out in the lonesome darkness, it was no trick at

all to imagine the bloodthirsty Count lying in wait for them, ready to spring, shrieking with mad laughter, from behind each bush or tree. The crunch of dead grasses under their feet made them start. Their eyes searched fearfully for movement in the windswept gloom, and their ears strained to catch every twig cracking.

"Shhh!" whispered Felix. "Hoof beats?"

He wasn't making it up. All of them could hear the gallop diminishing in the night. All of them felt the hairs stirring on the backs of their necks.

Sara shivered from head to toe. "It was j-just a story," she said, her teeth chattering. "Lord Doom isn't real. Anyway, he's in England."

As she tried to muster a shred of conviction, all the watery miles of the Atlantic offered little comfort. Prince Edward Island felt very much like England just then—and it was one of Lord Doom's favorite kind of nights.

"We could all be set upon by thieves, killed and buried! No one the wiser!" Felix cried as the ghastly thought jumped into his head.

It was Felicity who pushed them both onward in their hike.

"This is Avonlea, Felix," she commented sharply. "Not some lawless city."

Inside the lighthouse, Gus was helping his visitor from her hiding place, out of which she climbed very nimbly. He had already deduced her name from her pursuer's ranting.

"He's a mean piece of work, Miss Stone, that gentleman," Gus exclaimed indignantly as his guest untangled her skirts. He gestured towards the handy nook in the wall. "This is where Captain Crane used to stow rum and money."

The woman rushed to the window to peer fearfully into the night, exactly as Gus had done moments earlier.

"Rutherford's a monster," she cried passionately into the dark night landscape.

A trickle of blood had appeared on Gus's temple where the man, Rutherford, had struck him. Amanda Stone noticed it. Her hand flew to her lips in maidenly distress.

"Oh! You're bleeding. Oh! Oh!"

She snatched up Gus's fallen wool cap and pressed it tenderly to his wound. As she did so, her eyes became luminous with gratitude and her soft pink lips parted tremulously in concern.

"It's nothing, ma'am," Gus assured her stoutly, beginning to feel he would have gladly taken a dozen such wounds in her defense.

In fact, Gus couldn't stop staring. In his entire

life, he had never been even remotely this close to
so glamorous a creature. He had never heard silk
whisper so enchantingly with each tiny movement.
He had never breathed perfume as heady as a whiff
straight out of the Arabian Nights. He had never
gazed into feminine eyes that so clearly declared he
was a shining hero. Against such seductions,
honest, inexperienced Gus didn't stand a chance.
He gulped one more lungful of perfume—and fell
headlong into a hopeless infatuation.

Even when Amanda stopped daubing at his
forehead and dropped the wool cap, he found
himself unable to move. Amanda had noticed that
Gus was holding her missing shoe, which he had
picked up from the floor where Rutherford had
flung it. Hurriedly, she took the shoe and began to
cram her foot into it. Prince Edward Island, in
winter, was no place to be trotting about in
stockinged feet.

"I'd best be going," Amanda informed Gus
anxiously. "He might come back."

The prospect roused Gus like a gunshot.

"I'll take you directly to the constable, ma'am.
Let the law handle it."

This sensible suggestion only threw the much-
harried Miss Stone into greater consternation. Forgetting about her shoe, she clutched Gus by the arm.

"No, the law will take his side, even though I'm the innocent victim. Please, you must believe me."

With the full force of those pleading eyes fixed upon him, Gus would have believed her had she announced she was really a four-headed dodo bird in disguise. He grew even more agitated.

"But you can't go out into the night without protection!" Not if rude, bullying strangers were going to leap out of it and fling peaceful folk around!

Amanda finished slipping on her shoe and laid her soft hands on Gus's forearm. His concern seemed to touch her—and his intentions filled her with alarm.

"I beg you, sir, say nothing of this to anyone. Oh, it means my life," she added, packing her voice with painfully quivering significance.

Just then came the sound of footsteps at the door. Digger, forgotten in all this drama, began to bark again, causing Amanda to start. Fearing a return of her menacing nemesis, she immediately cowered into Gus's arms.

It was only the children, relieved to find Digger, thrusting themselves gratefully through the open door of the lighthouse. Once inside they stopped in their tracks, startled by the sate of riotous disarray. What's more, there was Gus, standing in the middle of it, half dressed, holding a gorgeous woman in his arms. Felicity, especially, went pale.

"Uh ..." began Gus.

Whatever he was about to stammer was interrupted by Amanda, who promptly kissed him, partly in gratitude, and partly to stop him from spilling the news about Rutherford's visit.

"Thank you for your courage and strength in my time of dire need," she breathed. "I feel certain we shall meet again."

With that, she slipped back out into the night and was gone before anyone could move. Dumfounded and totally agog, the children watched her vanish. Gus stood stock-still, a figure carved out of pure astonishment, only able to think of Amanda's kiss burning on his cheek.

"What'd she do that for?" asked Felix, with all the obtuseness of an eleven-year-old. He nearly got fried in the white-hot glare from his sister.

Amanda's kiss had done its work. Gus had room in his head only for what his alluring female visitor had wished, and he remained true to her wishes. So true that, a very short while later, the three children found themselves ejected from the lighthouse and trudging back towards the King farm, Digger trailing behind them. Sara was intrigued, Felix impressed and Felicity, quite visibly, furious.

"I wonder who she was," Sara mused, her eyes so bright with speculation that she completely forgot to worry about bloodthirsty nobles lying about in ambush.

Her reply was a hiss from Felicity. "Gus has some nerve, just turning us out into the night without a word of explanation!" Felicity had been white-lipped since the moment they had arrived at the lighthouse, but Sara couldn't see that in the dark. Nor could she leave off speculation.

"She was very beautiful. Where do you think Gus got that cut on his head?"

"Maybe he fell out of bed," Felix suggested, grinning.

"That woman probably knocked him on the head, then robbed him without him even noticing," Felicity exploded.

"Oh sure, then she kissed him, praised his courage and ran off into the night. Some robbery," Sara retorted, with more than a little sarcasm.

Felix hooted in agreement. "Of all the people you could choose to rob in Avonlea, Gus Pike is the last. He hasn't got anything at all. He's nobody important."

If ever there was a speech guaranteed to stir up Felicity King, this was it. Felicity had been a staunch defender of Gus from the moment he'd arrived in Avonlea. She heartily approved of his efforts to improve himself. And she hadn't forgotten how Gus had stood by her on a certain embarrassing evening when she had tried to pass herself off as a grown-up at an Avonlea party. In the aftermath, when she'd lamented that she'd grow up without ever being kissed, Gus had remedied the problem on the spot, with a smooch that came and went before Felicity knew what had happened to her. As a result, Felicity was far more of an admirer of Gus Pike than either Sara or Felix could possibly guess—and she turned heatedly on her brother.

"You just shut up about Gus Pike, Felix King. You don't know the first thing about it."

Felicity stormed off ahead, leaving Sara and Felix to look at each other in amazement.

Back in the lighthouse, Gus was still reeling from the events that had broken so rudely into his peaceful sleep. He'd tried tidying the mess Rutherford had left, but he soon found himself too distracted to remember where things were supposed to go. The only thing he felt capable of was going back to bed, where, perhaps, he might discover that everything had been part of some dream.

To this end, he retrieved his stocking cap, intending to pull it down over his ears. Much to his surprise, a small bag tumbled out of it and rolled onto the floor.

Slowly, Gus picked up the bag and shook the contents into his hand. Out came a fine linen handkerchief, strangely full of lumps and bumps. Untying the knot, Gus opened the cloth—and suddenly his palm seemed full of tumbling fire. From out of the handkerchief, a river of brilliantly flashing stones poured into his hand.

Gus stared at them, then at the handkerchief, which had elegantly embroidered initials — *A. S.* —in one corner. Slowly, a drift of perfume wafted up, seeming to warm the chilly air.

"Amanda Stone," he whispered, and he sat down hard, not sure what to make of anything that had happened to him that night.

Chapter Four

"Oh my goodness!" exclaimed Olivia Dale.

Jewels! Large, winking, many-colored jewels!

Olivia could be forgiven for gawking. As the

youngest of the grown-up Kings, she was often more like a friend to Sara and her cousins than an aunt. Before her recent marriage to Jasper Dale, she had actually lived at Rose Cottage with Sara and Hetty. Even after her marriage, she visited Rose Cottage so often that Sara didn't really feel her aunt had moved away at all. Olivia sat in the kitchen of Rose Cottage now, her cup of tea quite forgotten.

"It's a treasure," she whispered, blinking so hard at the astonishing sight that she didn't even have time to think how odd it was to see it in the kitchen of an Avonlea farmhouse.

Hetty, standing nearby, spared only a glance to see what was stirring her sister up so. Hetty, the eldest of the Kings, considered herself the head of the King clan. Unlike Olivia, who still bloomed with youth, Hetty was unmarried and well into middle age. She was a spare, bony woman with strong cheekbones and equally forceful opinions. Her hair was disciplined into a frighteningly neat bun and she wore a watch pinned to her bosom, as though to remind herself perpetually of precious moments awasting. She made it a point to be unimpressed by things that younger, more foolish heads were turned by.

"They're obviously not real, Olivia," Hetty said disparagingly. "Far too garish to be genuine."

Olivia, as romantic in her soul as Hetty was practical, took exception to this killjoy attitude.

"How do you know that?" she objected. "Why what if those rumors about old Captain Crane finding the treasure are true, Hetty?"

Avonlea had long been titillated by rumors of pirate's treasure hidden away in the many caves that riddled the coast. And the rumors might not have been so farfetched. Prince Edward Islanders had always been a seagoing people. Many had ancestors who might very well have been pirates, considering the old-time ideas of what was fair on the high seas. Hetty herself had an old diary that painted a less than respectable picture of some of her enterprising King forbears—a picture Hetty had done her best to suppress.

Hetty scoffed in her best schoolmarmish manner. Though he had been a good friend to Gus Pike, Hetty considered the Captain nothing but a half-crazy reprobate, good only for scaring children and ranting into the wind.

"Ezekiel Crane? That man couldn't find the sky lying face upwards on a raft in the middle of the Atlantic Ocean."

Just then, Gus Pike himself stepped out of the pantry. He'd been sent there to change into the snowy white shirt that now adorned his shoulders.

He was still fumbling at getting it done up as he came in.

"I never had no shirt with more than three buttons before," he told them, to explain his efforts. "Thanks, Miss Olivia. It's very fine."

Olivia glowed at Gus's pleasure. She had raced to finish the last cuff that very morning.

"Well, you know, Gus, it took me hardly any time at all with my new sewing machine."

Progress was inevitable, even in Avonlea. Olivia's new machine was quite a sensation in a community where everything was generally stitched by hand. Olivia's husband, Jasper, was a bit of an inventor, so it was natural that Olivia, too, should be in the forefront of new ideas. Hetty, on the contrary, supported tradition and examined the shirt with a critical eye.

"Let me see! Oh well, no substitute for my own fine hand-stitching, mind you." Hetty circled round and peered at the garment from the back, expecting to uncover some dread fault committed by the newfangled machine. She only found one committed by her sister. "But Olivia, what have you done? I never asked for an abrupt taper there."

She pointed to the shoulders, where Gus was beginning to develop a manly breadth. Olivia smiled to herself, knowing what pleased a growing fellow.

"Well, Hetty, Gus is a young man and he cuts a fine figure."

Gus grinned and Hetty sniffed. Making too much of oneself, Hetty believed, was a recipe for permanently addling one's head.

"Let us not forget that Gus's new employment is one of service, Olivia, not glamor," she commented, poking Gus in the ribs to make him stand up straighter.

"I'd never have gotten the job if it weren't for your letter of recommendation, Miss King," Gus put in gratefully.

In spite of all her prickles, Hetty had been responsible, almost single-handedly, for Gus's current elevation in life. Now she was helping him up the ladder by getting him a nice indoor job as a waiter at the nearby hotel. The new white shirt, the first Gus had ever had on his back, had been a joint project between Hetty and Olivia so that Gus could be properly dressed for his job.

"I'm sure you'll do very well at the White Sands, Gus," Olivia told him confidently, despite the fact that the White Sands was a very luxurious place. It attracted the fashionable and the wealthy from all over the continent to sample the bracing sea air and the glorious seaside vistas of Prince Edward Island. Before he met Hetty King, Gus wouldn't have dared so much as set foot upon the White Sands' lawn.

Hetty waved one of her hands dismissively. "Certainly he will. Now, off you go, boy. Remember 'Late for work, our duties will shirk.'"

"I'm halfway there already," Gus told her, then paused, his gaze sliding to the handkerchief in Olivia's hand. "Oh, Miss King, could you watch my treasure for me while I'm at work?"

Staunchly true to the wishes of Miss Amanda Stone, Gus had told no one about his adventure the previous night. He had resisted the children's wild inquiries and valiantly kept hidden the crazy turmoil her visit had set up inside him. Nevertheless, by the light of dawn, his first instinct had been to seek Hetty's help. If he couldn't tell her about Amanda, he could at least ask her to guard the booty he had found in his cap after Amanda had fled. That way he'd know the cache was safe and he wouldn't have to spend his first day at work wondering who was tearing up his humble home in his absence.

"Certainly I will," Hetty agreed, with an air of humoring the boy. With Gus in such a hurry, she didn't have time to deliver a lecture about making so much out of a handful of colored glass.

Reassured, Gus dashed for the door and set off hastily at a jog. Ever since Hetty had taken him to task about getting to school on time, Gus had developed a chronic fear of being late for anything. Consequently, he spent a good deal of his life on the run.

"He's certainly excited about that new job, isn't he?" Olivia observed, listening with pleasure to the sound of Gus's receding footsteps.

Hetty turned her attention to the table, from which she gathered up the handkerchief full of jewels.

"Treasure indeed," she muttered. "Although I suppose it wouldn't hurt to ascertain their actual worth. Yes, I'll take them to the jeweler in Carmody whilst I'm there."

Though she would never admit it out loud, Hetty was not as ready to dismiss Captain Crane as she appeared. She tucked the bundle onto the cupboard shelf and scanned the room.

"Olivia, you haven't seen my magazine, by any chance?"

The magazine, a copy of the very one Sara had been reading from the evening before, had just fallen into Olivia's hands. As Hetty searched, Olivia paged through it with increasing amusement.

"Oh? You mean 'Death Rides by Night'?" she inquired, her lips quirking.

Hetty's chin twitched righteously.

"I don't bother with serials, if that's what you're talking about. Oh no, just the occasional recipe and a political essay."

"Oh, of course," Olivia conceded, her lips on the very verge of knowing laughter.

Chapter Five

Gus raced all the way to the White Sands Hotel to make sure he wasn't late. He only slowed down when the establishment itself rose up in front of him, an imposing, half-timbered building set with utmost assurance amidst rolling grounds and prefaced by a wide circular drive. The lawns were lightly dusted with snow, and the whole scene was silhouetted against the broad white beaches from which the hotel had taken its name. Gus could not help but pause in awe, still not quite able to believe he actually had a job in the hotel's stylish interior.

This establishment was managed by one Percy Methley, the sort of man who made up for his obsequiousness to the guests by being a tyrant to his staff. Only a very glowing letter from Miss Hetty King had induced him to hire such a rough-edged unknown as young Gus Pike. When he saw Gus, red-faced from the outdoor air and hair windblown, he had more than a few second thoughts about his own reckless employment practices. Nevertheless, he marched Gus towards the dining room to begin work.

"It's simple enough, boy," he explained, in a tone that seriously doubted Gus's ability to comprehend. "You clear the dirty dishes off the tables and refill the coffee cups."

At the very entrance of the large room, he halted, irritated by the rushing of Gus's breath.

"Stop huffing, boy, you sound like an old train."

"I ran all the way, sir," Gus informed the manager virtuously as he hurried to tie on the waiter's apron the hotel had provided.

Mr. Methley, who hadn't had the benefit of being whipped into shape by Hetty King, was far from impressed.

"At the White Sands we don't confuse bustle with industry, Master Pike."

"Yes, sir," Gus agreed heartily, not understanding the dig.

The dining room was nearly filled with guests eating breakfast. They were a well-dressed crowd, the women in expensive, luxurious fabrics, the men in firmly tied cravats and jackets of good tweed. They looked as though they expected the best of service and would grow annoyed should it fall short.

Mr. Methley thrust a hot coffee pot into Gus's hands. "Get to it, then. The motto of the White Sands Hotel is: 'Guests shall have it before they know they want it.'"

Eager to succeed, Gus took Mr. Methley at his word. He immediately began filling the first cup he came to, even though the stout gentleman it belonged to risked scalded fingers in a vain effort to protect it.

"No lad, I don't want any," the man protested, only wanting to be left to his bacon and eggs in peace.

Gus only kept on pouring. Thanks to Mr. Methley, he already knew how to deal with anyone trying to resist the bounty of the White Sands Hotel.

"Well, mister, the idea is that you have it before you want it."

Gus left the cup brimming and the fellow in confusion. Then he went on to fill up cup after cup without the slightest reference to the wishes of their owners. Fortunately for Gus, his enthusiasm was generally ignored, and he soon was feeling pleased with himself indeed. His own shirt, he noted, was quite as resplendent as any the gentlemen wore under their fancy jackets. And maybe someday, if he worked very hard, he would own a fine jacket, too. He beamed with pride and began pouring coffee even more vigorously than before.

His progress around the dining room was so rapid that he soon found himself in front of a table where a slim female sat all alone. Not only was she alone, but her features were obscured by a long, dark veil. Obviously, she was breakfasting quietly by herself, sunk in deepest mourning.

"More coffee, ma'am?" Gus asked diffidently, having at last come upon a guest he was afraid to approach. Who knew what a grief-distracted woman might do if she had coffee unexpectedly thrust upon her?

The woman answered not a word. Instead, she turned slightly towards Gus and slowly lifted the veil from her face. Gus almost dropped the coffee pot. He found himself staring at his visitor from the night before—Amanda Stone. She was even more beautiful in the light of day. And she turned imploring eyes upon him.

"Please," she begged, her voice softly urgent, "show nothing in your face, brave Master Pike—my enemy is nearby. Act naturally."

All Gus could think of to do was pour some coffee into her cup, though he certainly didn't do it very naturally. His hand shook so much that the cup rattled and dark drops splashed out into the saucer.

"Did you get what I left you last night?" Amanda asked anxiously.

Even as Gus opened his mouth to reply, Amanda rushed a finger to her lips.

"Say nothing," she cautioned, apparently afraid Gus was going to blurt his answer to the entire dining room.

Catching her meaning, Gus nodded.

Amanda relaxed. Then, seeming to remember herself, her lashes began to flutter pathetically, hypnotizing Gus.

"It is the last vestige of my family's fortune. The man who was following us works for my late father's lawyer. I am an orphan ..."

"I'm near orphaned myself ..." Gus put in. His father was a thorough scoundrel who had once tried to kidnap Gus onto the high seas and involve him in a life of crime. Gus never wanted to see him again as long as he lived.

"Shhh!" Amanda whispered, determined to continue with her own story. "When my dear father died, the lawyer took the opportunity to take everything, including my mother's jewels. Well, I stole them back, and now Rutherford has been sent to bring them—and me—back. He intends that I should stand trial for taking what has been in my family for generations! I am desperate! I have nowhere to go. No one to turn to. Will you help me once again? Dear Master Pike?"

Who could resist such an appeal! The tale was just about as wrenching as anything a magazine serial could produce. And, to boot, it was reinforced by a cloud of gardenia perfume that affected Gus as powerfully as an intoxicating drug. Unable to take his eyes from the lovely creature begging his aid, Gus bobbed his head.

Amanda leaned closer. "Meet me after sunset in the old cemetery. Do you know it?"

Gus nodded a second time, so bedazzled he did not even wonder why anyone, especially a woman as refined as Amanda appeared to be, would choose as a meeting place a cemetery after dark.

Satisfied that she had gained her object, Amanda now looked anxiously around at the other guests, some of whom were glancing her way.

"Oh," she advised, "now it would be best if you continued as though nothing has happened."

Granting Gus a last, sad smile, Amanda dropped the veil again. Only then did Gus see Mr. Methley frowning sharply from the doorway and beckoning Gus over. Didn't Gus know it was absolutely forbidden for the staff to strike up conversations with the guests?

Gulping, Gus started towards the manager. He got most of the way there before his feet stopped moving. A hard, menacing presence had just walked into the room—Rutherford himself. Rutherford appeared even taller and harder than he had in the dark. And what's more, he had the temerity to stride across the dining room and seat himself at Amanda's table.

Rutherford sneered at Amanda's trailing veil. "You don't really think that old widow disguise could fool me, did you?" he jibed, in a voice only Amanda could hear.

For someone who had been pursued within an inch of her life mere hours before, Amanda seemed strangely unperturbed by his nearness. In fact, for one supposed to be in deep mourning, her tone was unaccountably smug.

"I haven't got the gems, Robert," she informed him.

Gus saw only that Amanda was being harassed. Ignoring Mr. Methley's furious motions and a number of guests asking for coffee, Gus began gallantly working his way back to Amanda's table.

"Perhaps not, Amanda," Rutherford was saying, "but never forget. I'm like your shadow—patient, dark and impossible to avoid."

Amanda only lifted a brow, archly.

"Have you considered, Robert, that shadows are also predictable and insubstantial and thus ... harmless?"

The remark was calculated to annoy, and it succeeded admirably. Rutherford began to scowl.

"I think you know my capabilities. Perhaps you won't be quite so pretty when I'm done with you."

Gus was close enough to hear this last threat. His young face registered the shock. He had to do something to help the lady in distress. Unfortunately, he had no sword or mace with which to defend her—only a half-filled coffee pot.

"More coffee, ma'am?" Gus asked, determined to make the best of the means at hand. He moved to pour coffee into Amanda's cup but made sure the scalding liquid splashed instead over Rutherford's arm. With a curse, Rutherford leaped up, knocking Gus backward and—oh, tragedy of tragedies—sloshing coffee from the pot all over Gus's new white shirt.

"Oh you stupid, clumsy...! What a ..."

Rutherford stopped to scrutinize Gus, suddenly realizing where he had seen him before.

"You're the lighthouse brat, aren't you?"

"Leave her be," Gus warned him, with all the ferocity his honest soul could muster. Rutherford was half again as big and almost twice as old as he was.

Rutherford snatched up a napkin to blot his coffee-soaked wrist. As he did so, his lip curled at Amanda.

"Getting a little desperate for allies, aren't you?" he jeered, jerking his head towards Gus.

As far as Amanda was concerned, the fray was getting out of hand. Not bothering to answer Rutherford, she rose from the table, gathered her skirts and made a prudent retreat from the dining room. Rutherford would have been on her heels had not Mr. Methley thrust himself into his path. Horrified at what had just happened, the manager was almost turning himself inside-out with apology.

"The hotel is extremely sorry for any inconvenience and I assure you—"

"Fine, fine," Rutherford spat, eager to be off. "Just keep this stripling away from me."

Mr. Methley turned his furious eye on Gus. This

clumsy busboy would feel the force of his wrath.

"Of course. He's relieved of his duties immediately."

The manager began shoving Gus towards the door. Gus glared at Rutherford even as he pulled his hot, dripping shirt away from his skin. With everyone staring at him, Gus made a last effort to retain some dignity.

"We'll meet again, sir," he flung out bravely.

Rutherford looked down at Gus. "You'd better hope not, boy."

Mr. Methley jerked Gus into the corridor, whence he was very shortly thrust, stripped of his apron and unemployed, outside into the cold.

Chapter Six

Gus's career as a waiter had collapsed after only twenty minutes on the job. After his ignominious ejection from the White Sands, Gus retired, discouraged, to the lighthouse to mull over the matter and try to get the coffee stains out of his precious new shirt. Felix spotted him trudging home and decided to drop in on him, determined to find out why Gus was home so early.

Back at the lighthouse, Felix heard the sad tale

of Gus's dismissal. He picked up the newspaper and started scanning the want ads. Pretending to smoke Gus's unlit pipe, Felix felt much less perturbed than Gus about the firing.

"How's your arithmetic? You could be a clerk at the Carmody bank," Felix suggested, pointing to a printed notice. Gus had to have some kind of job or he would starve before their very eyes.

"All right till I run out of fingers," Gus grunted glumly. "Miss King will never let me hear the end of it, losing that job. And on the first day."

Added to her dismay over the lost job would be her reaction when she saw what had happened to the fine new shirt Olivia had worked so hard to make him. Gus bent over a sudsy basin, trying with all his might to scrub out the coffee blotches, but he was only making the problem worse.

"She'll understand it was an accident," Felix suggested, in an effort to be reassuring. Then, in answer to a disgusted look from Gus, Felix had to shake his head. "No, I guess not."

After several minutes of rustling the paper and chewing on the stem of Gus's pipe, Felix got to his true mission.

"C'mon, Gus, you gotta tell me what's going on. If you don't, Felicity will pluck out my eyelashes one by one."

Felix wasn't going to confess that he, too, was consumed with curiosity about the scene he had witnessed the previous night. And it certainly wasn't like Gus to lose a good job the first morning he tried it.

Mention of Felicity only made Gus think of all things right and proper. He noticed the pipe between Felix's teeth.

"Put that away, Felix. Miss King says smoking at a tender age indicates vulgarity."

Gus himself had been smoking since a very tender age and hadn't had the advantage of a Hetty King to stop the habit before it was too late. He took another slap at the shirt, then dropped it back into the basin in defeat.

"I should have known you was sent to scout me out. My lips are sealed tight as the Pyramids. It's a question of a lady's honor and safety," Gus declared, unconsciously thrusting out his chest.

Felix was too young comprehend the snares that beauty might lay in the path of a susceptible lad on the verge of manhood. He only understood that some strange woman was making Gus clam up in front of his real friends.

"Just because she's pretty ..."

"She's the most beautiful woman I've ever seen," Gus confessed in a rush, not even bothering with the consequences should Felix carry this remark back to Felicity. His eyes lost their focus. For one long, dreamy moment he looked as though he actually saw the enchanting Amanda seated on a cloud before him. With difficulty, he shook himself back to reality, and the shirt, with its ruinous brown blotches, awash in the bottom of the basin.

"Maybe there's some miracle mixture at Lawson's that'd clean out this stain," he muttered, somewhat hopelessly.

Gus set out at once for the general store, plodding along with his old scarf flung around his neck and the damp shirt clutched in his hand. If he could get the stains out before Hetty found out about the lost job, he would have managed to rescue at least one of the favors she had done for him.

Gus's mind was so distracted by his own concerns that he scarcely noticed when he entered the village. Nor did he expect anyone else to notice him, for Avonlea was a close-knit village with fixed ideas about who belonged where. As an outsider, not related to a single soul, and a penniless drifter working at the fish cannery, he was right down at the bottom of the social scale, and a number of people didn't even bother to say hello to him.

The Potts family belonged in this category. So, if Gus wasn't aware of people on the street suddenly swinging round to stare at him as he passed, he was certainly stopped short when Sally Potts dashed out of the Potts house and skipped to a halt in front of him.

"Gus!" Sally cried, as though greeting a long-lost relative. She was actually coatless in the cold in her hurry to catch him.

"Afternoon, Sally Potts," Gus answered warily.

Sally's mother was one of the worst gossips in Avonlea, and Sally could be nasty when she wanted. In school, Gus had smarted more than once from her jeering tongue, and he tried to figure out what sort of trick she was up to this time.

"We would most surely be honored by your presence at Sunday dinner, Mr. Pike," Sally chirped, bobbing a fetching little curtsy as she spoke.

The idea of Gus being invited into the Potts house was about the same as his being asked to call on the mayor of Charlottetown.

"At your house? Me?"

Sally nodded vigorously, eyes wide and innocent. "Of course, Gus. Mother has made a special occasion of it. We're having stuffed goose."

The stuffed goose story clinched it. Only on holidays did the frugal souls in Avonlea kill and cook a goose. And when they did, they didn't tease poor working lads with hints of getting a taste of it.

Gus squared his jaw. "I'm not in no mood for jokes, Sally Potts." And he hurried off, leaving Sally shivering in the breeze behind him.

Vainly, she waved her arms. "But, Gus ... it's with all the trimmings ..."

Now Gus began to realize that women were nodding and men tipping their hats as he walked along. Once he even peeked behind himself, thinking some important person was walking in his trail. And to top this wonder off, Mr. Methley came rushing up to him in the street.

"Master Pike! Master Pike! A moment of your time?"

Automatically, Gus braced for another tongue-lashing. "Don't worry—I didn't take no silverware with me."

Methley, who had that very morning chucked Gus out of the White Sands, laughed as though the boy were the wit of the season.

"Nonsense, nonsense," Mr. Methley boomed. "All a misunderstanding. I hope you won't hold it against the hotel, Master Pike."

"But you just fired me!" Gus insisted, wondering whether Mr. Methley had been into the hotel's cooking sherry.

Mr. Methley smiled as warmly as his commercial soul would allow.

"We'd like to extend to you a complimentary suite—at least until you're able to find more suitable accommodations."

Gus's jaw almost fell off its hinges.

"What?"

"A person of your stature is exactly the sort the White Sands must cultivate," the manager purred, as though Gus's frayed jacket and cracked boots were just the thing to spruce up the hotel corridors. "A very good day to you, Master Pike."

Tipping his hat, Mr. Methley marched off, leaving a very mixed-up Gus standing in the road.

Cautiously, Gus slipped into the general store. Surely, people would act normally in there.

Mrs. Lawson immediately abandoned the customer she had been serving and rushed over, smiling. It seemed to make no difference that the customer she had abandoned was Mrs. Potts, the very woman Sally claimed was planning to cook a stuffed goose dinner for Gus.

"Gus, how nice to see you! Can we do something for you?"

The last thing Gus expected was special attention, especially when a number of women were standing there, waiting their turns. He had already stepped to the notice board to see whether there were any jobs advertised. Taken aback, he looked at the other customers, expecting annoyance. But instead, they were all nodding and beaming, as though it were perfectly natural Gus should be served first. Gus cleared his throat and held out the garment knotted in his hand.

"I was wondering if you had a shirt-cleaner that cleans stains of a stubborn sort, that don't cost too much."

Gus had to watch every penny, especially now that he was out of work. Mrs. Lawson fluttered her fingers.

"Don't concern yourself with cost. Your credit is good here."

"It is?"

This was certainly news. Up until then, Gus had yet to meet anyone in Avonlea willing to extend five cents' credit to him. Gus was more perplexed than ever!

Eventually, Gus emerged from the store with a small paper bag of stain-remover in his hand and wonderment stamped on his face. Since kind Mrs. Lawson was not at all the sort to get involved in unpleasant jokes, Gus could only assume that they had all taken leave of their senses. Until their sanity returned, he had the stain-remover to try and a credit account started in the store.

Shrugging, he stepped round to the back of the building, meaning to take a shortcut to the lighthouse. But no sooner had he passed from the street than he found himself seized by the neck and slammed up against the stack of barrels behind him. His assailant was the muscular and nefarious Rutherford.

"You are out of your league in conflict with your betters," Rutherford snarled. "So tell me where the gems are or I'll break your arm."

Rutherford must have figured out that there was only one place the lady could have left her valuables—and that was at the lighthouse. After his initial gasp, Gus shut his mouth tight, ready to face the worst Rutherford could do rather than betray the trust of the fair Amanda. Rutherford, towering over Gus, jerked him higher against the barrels and started to twist his arm. A sudden growling made him turn. It was Digger to the rescue, appearing out of nowhere, pursuing his grudge against the man who had kicked him. Out in the open, though, Digger's idea of ferocity only seemed to amuse Rutherford.

"You'd need a lot sharper teeth than that to frighten me!" he told the dog, looking as if he might aim another kick.

Giving up on direct intimidation, Digger began

to bark at the top of his lungs to summon help. Felix came running around the corner.

"Digger! Digger!"

At the sight of Rutherford and Gus, Felix screeched to a halt. A couple of other people, attracted by the commotion, craned their necks around the side of the store, forcing Rutherford to let go of his victim. As more people gathered, Rutherford decided it was time to beat a retreat. His eyes bored into Gus.

"She'll play you for a fool just like every other man or boy in long pants who catches her fancy."

With this parting shot, Rutherford strode away, the cape of his coat swirling angrily around his shoulders. As for Gus, he was far too relieved to think about what Rutherford had just said, or even wonder whether Rutherford himself might have been played for a fool. He only grabbed Digger and patted him gratefully for the rescue.

Chapter Seven

As night approached, Gus forgot all about the strange deference with which he had been treated in Avonlea. He forgot his stained shirt, too, for he had something much more urgent on his mind. He had to get the gems back from Hetty so that he could pass them on to Amanda, keeping the promise he had so recklessly made that morning at the White Sands.

However, getting such items back from Hetty without a very good explanation proved a much stickier task than Gus had bargained for. He no sooner got to Rose Cottage than Hetty plopped him down into a chair at the kitchen table and poured him a cup of tea he hadn't the least desire for. And, despite Gus's best efforts, she didn't let him get a word in edgewise. She was too excited herself about her news.

"It's a fortune," she gloated. "The jeweler in Carmody couldn't say exactly what your jewels are worth. Silly man just held them in his hand and giggled. It was ridiculous."

It was a measure of how much Gus was mesmerized by Amanda that Hetty's news barely registered. He kept his eyes on his teacup throughout Hetty's exclamations. Finally, after a scalding gulp, he managed to state his mission.

"I want them back, Miss King."

Hetty spread her palms and shook her head at the boy's unbelievable foolishness. Did he think valuable jewels dropped from trees every day!

"Oh no. They're securely locked up in the post

office safe, where they will remain until we can consult a solicitor and have them properly deposited in an account for you."

"But they were given to *me*, Miss King," Gus objected, dismayed at seeing his own affairs so abruptly snatched from his hands.

Hetty flung him a disapproving look.

"Oh my, so you'd be an idler, would you, Gus Pike? Well, I'll have you know, a gadabout with money is a gadabout just the same."

Since Hetty had taken on Gus as her reclamation project, she felt she was in charge not only of his education and deportment but of his moral development as well. A mere fortune in jewels would not sway her from her principles.

Gus, who had been a little spoiled after all by the attention lavished upon him in Avonlea, unwisely tried another approach.

"Well, Miss King, everyone else is being nice to me, I don't see why you can't be too."

"Because I'm no fair-weather friend, Gus Pike, that's why. Lord, if you can't handle a job pouring coffee, how on earth are you going to handle a fortune in gems? Hmm? No, no, they'll all stay in the post office safe, and that's final!" Hetty thumped the table to emphasize her decision.

Defeated, Gus sighed deeply and slumped in

his chair. Not even noticing, Hetty reached for the plate of refreshments.

"Go on," she urged, full of satisfaction at her victory, "cake!"

Over in the King farmhouse, Sara Stanley wasn't having much success in her attempt to learn domestic skills. In charge of dinner that night, she had concocted a stew in which unpeeled, undercooked potatoes swam in an unappetizing, grayish liquid. As she served it up at the kitchen table, Felix, Felicity and Cecily exchanged doubtful looks. Only Digger devoured his share enthusiastically, from a pot on the floor.

"I despair at your cooking abilities, Sara Stanley," Felicity informed her in grim tones. An inability to cook was a terrible disadvantage for any Avonlea girl.

Sara pressed her lips into a rather thin line. "How can I concentrate on reading a recipe properly when you make me read that magazine aloud all day?"

The magazine lay on the sideboard. The children had followed Lord Doom through several bouts of mayhem between breakfast and supper that day. They were all fervently thankful not to be anywhere near his estate.

"Let's go ask Gus to take us all for a fancy dinner at the White Sands!" suggested Felix, eyeing his plateful distastefully. "He can afford it."

Hetty hadn't been able to keep her visit to Carmody to herself. News of Gus's newfound wealth in jewels had reached the King farm just before lunch, which certainly explained the strange behavior of the folk in Avonlea. Felicity, whose mind still burned with the scene she had witnessed in the lighthouse between Gus and Amanda, twisted in her chair.

"Gus Pike will soon forget all about his old friends, now that's he's rich, you just see if he doesn't," she predicted scathingly.

"Are you mad at poor Gus, Felicity?" Cecily asked, with such innocence and accuracy that Felicity could only stiffen in her chair.

Digger gulped the last of his stew, cocked one ear and suddenly began to scratch at the door, asking to get out.

Felix grinned at his older sister. "She's conceived by jealousy."

"She's *consumed* by jealousy," Sara corrected, giggling over the sudden flare of heat in Felicity's cheeks.

"I'm no such thing, Sara Stanley," Felicity shot back vehemently. "I'm just trying to be

Gus's friend. Don't you all see that Gus is in some sort of trouble? I've no doubt that woman is behind it all."

The spectacle of Felicity, red-faced and sputtering, so distracted Cecily that she reached behind her and, without thinking, opened the door for Digger. Instantly, the dog was gone into the night.

"Oh no! Digger!" Cecily groaned when she realized what she had done.

"Cecily!"

Felicity jumped up in annoyance. Horrible pictures of Mr. Armstrong and his shotgun leapt into everyone's minds. Without even having to discuss it, they all abandoned the table and started grabbing their coats.

"What about dinner?" Sara wanted to know. Her normally ravenous cousins seemed all too happy to leave her proud creation congealing on their plates.

The children were already streaming out of the door. Sara had to scramble for her own coat and race to keep up with them. Only Cecily was barred.

"I know," Cecily sighed. "Stay here in case Digger comes back. Which he never does."

Chapter Eight

Gus, unable to retrieve the bag of gems from Hetty's keeping, had to proceed, empty-handed, to his promised rendezvous with Amanda in the old cemetery. The cemetery was not a place anyone would choose to visit voluntarily, even by daylight. It hadn't been used for years. Brush had crept amongst the gravestones, and tree branches hung low, plucking at those who passed underneath. A desolate gloom seemed to hang in the very air.

A chill, damp wind moaned in from off the water, making twigs rattle and tree branches scrape against each other. Gus, carrying a lantern, had had to stumble through brambles and step over gravestones to reach a relatively level spot. When he hung the lantern from a tree branch, it cast an inadequate yellow glow by which he paced nervously and rubbed his hands together in an effort to keep warm. The fact that he was there at all was testimony to his courage and his infatuation with Amanda. As the wind gusted erratically, heralding a storm, Gus shivered inside his jacket. He fervently hoped it was only Amanda he was going to meet in such a spooky place.

A crack behind him made him start.

"Miss Stone?" he called out, peering into the blackness. "Miss Stone?"

Though he got no answer, he was convinced something was there. He squared his young shoulders valiantly.

"If that's you, Rutherford, come out and face me!" Considering that Rutherford could pick him up and toss him with one hand, this challenge showed quite a lot of bravado on Gus's part.

The crackle came again, this time closer. As Gus pushed a branch back, a form came flying out of the darkness and knocked him backwards, sprawling on the ground. Luckily for Gus, the figure was furry all over and intent only on licking his face. Gus laughed aloud with sheer relief.

"Digger! Digger! Come to keep me company? That's a boy."

As Gus scratched Digger's ears in rough camaraderie, Amanda herself stepped into the circle of lantern light. Gus leapt hurriedly to his feet. How could she just appear like that, out of nowhere?

Amanda and Digger weren't Gus's only audience. From only a few gravestones away, other eyes observed the scene. Eyes that belonged to Felix, Sara and Felicity, who were crouching down behind a large, crumbling monument. Drawn by

Digger's flight and the glow of the lantern, the children had stumbled upon the scene in the cemetery and taken cover. Scarcely daring to breathe, they listened to every word between Gus and Amanda.

"Why does Digger always go straight for Gus at night?" Sara whispered. This was the second time that Digger had dragged them through the dark over to the boy.

"Gus always had lots of fish guts around," Felix supplied.

"So?"

"Digger loves to roll in them."

The two girls made a face.

Several yards away, Amanda glided warily towards Gus. "Is it safe?" she inquired, tremulously.

Affected by her nearness, Gus struck a stalwart pose. "That Rutherford fella tried to scare me off of helping you. But I ain't afraid of him."

Amanda's eyes opened wide in what appeared to be genuine alarm.

"You should be afraid of Rutherford, Gus. Oh, but I appreciate your help and your trust."

"Why, just by the looking a man can see you are a woman of virtue and kindness," Gus declared, turning pink with pleasure.

❧❧❧

"Oh, please hide me, I'm in grave danger
and there isn't much time."

❧❧❧

"Please," Amanda begged, her voice
softly urgent, "show nothing in your face,
brave Master Pike — my enemy is nearby."

കൈരൂ

"Your are out of your league in conflict
with your betters," Rutherford snarled. "So tell me
where the gems are or I'll break your arm."

❦❦❦

"You can't arrest no one," Gus intervened.
"Oh no, boy?" Rutherford, with obvious relish,
brandished a large metal badge in all their faces.
"I'm with the McGrath Detective Agency of Boston..."

Amanda approached Gus alluringly and placed light fingers on his shoulder. Gus turned pinker still and didn't know what to do with his hands.

Crouched behind the gravestone, Felicity seethed. "If she's a woman of virtue then I'm the Queen of Sheba!"

"He'll rue the day he messes with Gus Pike, I tell ya," Gus announced, quite unhinged by Amanda's inebriating gaze. And no wonder. When Amanda fluttered her lashes so fetchingly, the toughest renegade could have been forgiven for taking leave of his senses.

"Oh, I don't doubt it!" she breathed, fairly melting with admiration of Gus's manly fortitude. "But if you'll just give me the gems, then I can escape to the mainland tonight."

There were ships to be caught, even at that late hour, for those who knew where to find them—and Amanda was in a tearing hurry. She barely restrained her impatience as she waited for Gus to produce the gems from his pocket. Swallowing hard, Gus had to admit his failure.

"Oh, they're locked up at the post office, locked up in the safe, Miss Stone. I'll get them for you tomorrow."

Amanda barely managed to stifle a cry of disappointment and frustration. Gus was still in possession of her treasure. So long as he had the gems, Amanda was in Gus's power.

"The jewels are hers!" Sara whispered from her hiding place.

"Rutherford thwarts me at every turn!" Amanda lamented, actually looking as though she were going to tear her artistically coiffed hair. She was behaving as though Rutherford had been the one to put the jewels in the post office safe.

"No, no," explained Gus, "it's Miss Hetty King that's the thwarter." Then, passionately, he declared, "I'll do whatever it takes to help you, Miss Stone!"

That helping Amanda might involve being mangled by the ferocious Rutherford seemed not to bother Gus one whit. It was almost worth coming without the jewels tonight if it meant the delectable Miss Stone was going to hang on his every word like that.

"See how noble Gus is?" Sara said to her companions. She prided herself on having spotted Gus's fine qualities the first time she saw him in Avonlea.

Felicity clenched her jaw, unimpressed. "He's smitten is what he is!"

"Until tomorrow then," Amanda murmured to Gus. "But Master Pike, be on your guard. Tangling with Rutherford might mean you leaving Avonlea forever!"

Gus did not shrink from this drastic prospect. Everything precious to him in Avonlea was whirled clean out of his head by Amanda's tantalizing proximity. Visions of himself defending the lady as she fled from refuge to refuge clutching her family heirlooms quite swept him away.

"If I was with you, I wouldn't mind a bit!"

At this blatant defection, Felicity gasped aloud. And she gasped again as Amanda sidled even closer and planted a whopping kiss on Gus's ardent, love-struck face as a reward for his gallantry. Sara was dumbstruck and, as for Felix, Felicity tried unsuccessfully to clamp her hands over his saucer-sized eyes.

"The tramp!" Felicity exploded, "taking advantage of poor Gus like that."

"He doesn't seem to be struggling," Sara commented as Gus remained motionless in Amanda's grip.

Felix was awestruck.

"He must be breathing through his ears," he squeaked, wondering how Gus could be kissed like that and still get oxygen.

Finally, Amanda released a wobbly Gus and disappeared into the night.

Felicity sprang to her feet, the light of battle blazing in her eye. Obviously, if Gus couldn't look after himself with scheming seductresses, someone else was going to have to do it for him.

"I'm going to follow that hussy and demand she leave Gus alone!"

As Felicity raged off after Amanda, Sara recovered enough of her senses to realize that Felicity needed a cohort. In her present state of mind, Felicity might have a go at tearing Amanda limb from limb!

"Felix, you stay with Gus!" Sara ordered hurriedly.

Before Felix could so much as open his mouth in protest, Sara had also dashed away into the darkness. Felix was in no way equipped to deal with matters of the heart, Sara felt, and it was best he not mix himself in them at all. Generously, she left the dog to keep Felix company.

Felix screwed up his face. "All this skull and daggery and no supper ..."

Digger suddenly turned and began to growl at the cemetery gate. A flash of lightning illuminated a horse and rider galloping into the burying ground. The stark silhouette so resembled the illustration in the magazine the children had been reading that Felix felt his heart get ready to drop out.

The snorting horse was being driven hard. It almost ran Gus down before it could be pulled to a halt near the lantern. By the light, Gus could see that the cloaked figure was Rutherford, brandishing the heavy stick he always carried in his hand. The horse was so spooked by nearly slamming into Gus that it began to rear and plunge, threatening to pitch off its rider. Rutherford recognized Gus at once and began to wave the stick furiously.

"I'm out of patience, boy. Out of my way!"

Gus stumbled off balance among the roots and brush of the cemetery. But when he regained his feet, he stood firm, actually trying to grasp at the bridle of Rutherford's horse. Rutherford had clearly come in pursuit of Amanda, and Gus intended to stop him on the spot.

"Come down off there," he challenged recklessly, still drunk from Amanda's kiss. "Let's go at it, man to man!"

"You're a thick-skulled whelp," Rutherford shouted back. And to prove it, he struck Gus a resounding smack across the head with his stick. Though the pain made Gus stagger, the courageous lad did not give up his ground. Rutherford lifted his arm, getting ready to slash down a second time.

But before he could, Digger exploded from the darkness and sank his fangs into the attacker's boot. Swearing, Rutherford kicked the dog away and spurred his horse, making Gus once again leap aside to avoid being trampled. The horse's powerful shoulder knocked Gus sideways down to the rough earth. In a moment, Rutherford was galloping off into the darkness—in exactly the same direction Amanda had gone.

Felix came running out from behind the gravestone to where Gus lay sprawled.

"Oh Gus, are you all right?"

Gus stumbled to his feet, shaking his head from the pain of the blow. Digger leapt at his knees, trying to lick his face.

"What are you doing here?" Gus asked, astonished to see Felix in such a deserted place at such an hour.

Felix was too shaken up to be other than perfectly honest.

"Spying on you while Felicity and Sara watch your friend," he told Gus, spilling everything at a single go.

Urgency flooded Gus as he realized which way Rutherford was going. "I have to go warn Amanda." He started off, expecting Felix to follow.

"But I haven't had any supper tonight," Felix complained, seeing himself about to be drawn into another unfed expedition that had nothing at all to do with himself.

"I promised I'd protect her with my life." Gus's words cried shame to anyone so crass as to think of his stomach when such high purpose called.

Holding his bruised head with one hand and the lantern with the other, Gus was soon bounding away among the gravestones. Felix either had to go with him or stay by himself in the pitch-black, stormy cemetery. The wind shook skeleton branches, reminding Felix of the many real skeletons buried just beneath his feet.

"You didn't promise her *my* life," Felix yelled out reproachfully, starting after Gus as fast as his young legs would carry him.

Had Gus but known enough to stay at the lighthouse instead of hanging about graveyards, he could have collected Amanda's jewels for her that night after all. After he had left Rose Cottage in defeat that afternoon, Hetty and Olivia had exchanged words over the matter of possession. The outcome of this somewhat heated discussion was that Hetty and Olivia, clutching a lantern between them, were marching as fast as they could along the path towards the lighthouse.

"Hetty, returning the gems to Gus is the right thing to do," Olivia said encouragingly as they stumbled over half-frozen clods of earth and avoided slippery tongues of snow.

Unable to prevent herself from casting fearful glances over her shoulder, Hetty had other concerns. Like the children, she had tales of Lord Doom percolating in her head. She wouldn't put it past the fellow to spring out of the blackberry bushes, red-eyed as a newt, ravening for flesh.

"Two women ... a handful of jewels ... in the middle of the night: it's absurd! How did I let you talk me into this ... ridiculous gesture?"

"Hetty, if you treat Gus as a responsible adult he'll behave responsibly," Olivia argued.

Their speed had taken them right to the lighthouse steps, where Olivia hammered on the door, first politely, then urgently. The windows were dark and not a movement was heard inside.

"Oh, I don't believe he's home," Olivia said, disappointed.

"Well, I suppose we could leave him a note," Hetty suggested sardonically. "'Dear Gus, your treasure is hidden here beneath the door mat.' Of course, he doesn't even have a doormat."

The two women looked at each other, stuck with a fortune in jewels in their pockets and no place to leave it. Olivia brightened with a sudden idea.

"I know. We'll just keep them for him overnight."

"We will?" The lantern twitched in Hetty's hand as she contemplated babysitting such valuables stones. "I shan't sleep a wink. Oh, where is that dratted boy anyway?"

"Hetty, you worry too much. This is Avonlea, not some wild place full of thieves. Come on."

Hetty resolved to keep them under her pillow. For certain, no thief would disturb them there.

Apprehensively, the two started back along the murky path, which, seen from a deserted lighthouse with the sea rolling in below, might very well have been peopled with mad counts intent on wreaking havoc. Flickers of lightning from the impending storm only served to throw the leafless trees into relief against the purple sky. At a growl of thunder, the two woman doubled their pace. Then a distant, wolfish howl, probably from a lonely farm dog, caused them both to jump with nerves, give in to their terrors and start running back towards Rose Cottage just as fast as they could drag their skirts behind them.

Chapter Nine

At the White Sands Hotel, nearly all of the guests had gone to bed, leaving the lobby drowsy and deserted. Only a few lamps were left burning, in case of latecomers.

Amanda Stone certainly was a latecomer. She rushed into the lobby, breathless, red-cheeked and already unloosing the cloak from her shoulders as she pressed on the desk bell for service. As she waited, she peered apprehensively towards the entrance behind her. Anyone watching her would have sworn she feared a pursuer thumping in after her through the heavy oak doors. Yet the moment Mr. Methley appeared, clad in his robe, Amanda calmed her agitation and turned on her charm.

"Oh, I'm so sorry, Mr. Methley, the hour being so late ... but I'm afraid I need my key."

The White Sands did not allow the guests to carry its ornate keys about with them. Instead, they were kept in slots behind the desk, available when needed. Amanda was so picturesque that Mr. Methley merely smiled and turned to the key slots.

"We're here only to serve, Miss Stone," he murmured, just as though he enjoyed nothing so much as being roused from his own fireside on cold, stormy nights in order to get late guests their keys. He handed Amanda the room key, then paused. "That certain Mr. Rutherford was asking after you earlier this evening. He ... I told him you'd gone out. He seemed most anxious to speak with you."

The mere mention of Rutherford caused Amanda to tighten. She had kept him from catching up to her until now, and she meant to keep him off her trail as much as possible. To this end, she assumed a pose of delicately distressed helplessness. She was, after all, supposed to be in mourning.

"Oh, I don't want to see him, Mr. Methley. I'm afraid I can't deal with lawyers and bankers now. Please, you do understand. I need quiet, time to reflect."

Gus wasn't the only male susceptible to Amanda's charms. One glance into her tragic eyes and even hard-nosed Mr. Methley fell for her plea, hook, line and sinker.

"Of course, Miss Stone. Of course."

"Thank you."

The manager actually patted Amanda's hand for reassurance. His reward was a grateful, melting glance from under those long lashes as Amanda took the key and hurried upstairs. Mr. Methley stood gazing after her until her voluminous skirts had vanished from sight. Then, with a sigh, he returned to his own quarters, leaving the lobby to silence again.

However, no sooner had Mr. Methley settled down into his favorite chair than Felicity and Sara charged into the hotel, bringing a gust of cold air and a great deal of indignation with them. Felicity was bristling all over with outrage and steely determination, and Sara was out of breath from chasing after her.

"Pease reconsider, Felicity," Sara begged, peering anxiously around her. "We don't even know what room she's in."

Felicity wasn't going to be put off by such a trifling obstacle. As imperiously as a duchess demanding service, she marched straight up to the desk and slammed her palm down on the bell. Sara jumped. Mr. Methley, still clad in his robe, hurried out eagerly, supposing the beguiling Miss Stone had forgotten something. When he saw who had disturbed him, peevish annoyance soured his face.

"What are you children doing here?"

Mr. Methley had no use at all for children—unless, of course, they were booked into the White Sands in the company of rich parents. Farm children running around loose after dark ought to be tossed out of the place bodily.

Fueled by her wrath, Felicity wasn't daunted by the manager's hostile look. She drew herself up to her full height and assumed a commanding tone to show him she was no child.

"Mr. Methley, I demand to know the room number of the woman who just came in here."

"You demand...?" Mr. Methley's brows shot up. He was amazed that anyone, much less two impertinent local girls, could expect him to violate the confidentiality of his guests. "Young lady, do your parents know where you are?"

Unwittingly, he had hit Felicity's weak spot. She had been left in charge of the household while her mother and father were absent and was expected to behave in a responsible manner. Alec and Janet King would have been horrified at the idea of Sara and Felicity traipsing about deserted cemeteries and hotel lobbies in the black of night. Felicity cast a desperate glance at Sara. Mr. Methley spotted it.

"Out!" he shouted, shooing them off with his hands. "Go home!"

Felicity was caught with her mouth open and no answer on her tongue—all of which left it up to Sara to save the day. Despite Sara's personal reservations about Felicity's actions, her first loyalty was to her cousin, and she stepped forward in an effort to help. Luckily, before she had come to live in Avonlea, Sara had traveled with her wealthy father and knew a thing or two about hotel managers.

"Mr. Methley," she said importantly, "I'm afraid we must speak to her. She's ..." Sara groped for a plausible excuse and grabbed the biggest she could find, "... she's in grave and immediate danger."

Mr. Methley, who had seen Amanda safe and well not ten minutes before, didn't budge.

"Write a note and I will deliver it," he told the girls, fixing them with beady, skeptical eyes.

Felicity showed signs of collapsing then and there. Sara, resourceful girl that she was, was only momentarily thrown off her stride.

"We must deliver the message personally," she insisted. And then, at Mr. Methley's obstinacy, she became even more emphatic. "It will reflect badly on the hotel if she is not warned. You could escort us upstairs."

Mr. Methley remained doubtful but could not help being affected by the air of urgency and authority the twelve-year-old girl managed to project. Besides, he didn't want any trouble at the White Sands that might possibly be construed as his fault. Better, he decided, to be safe than sorry.

"All right then, in that case," he finally agreed,

grudging and suspicious. "I will accompany you to her room."

As Mr. Methley set out ahead of them, Felicity shot Sara a look of naked admiration and gratitude. Not the least pleased at having had to resort to such methods, Sara only frowned back. As the two hurried up the curving stairs after the manager, Sara's eyes warned Felicity that this had better be the end of such uncomfortable subterfuges.

The two girls might have forgotten all about their own skulduggery in sheer wonder had they been able to see what was going on in Amanda's room. Instead of retiring demurely as a respectable lady should at such an hour, Amanda stood in front of her mirror tucking a shovel cap over her knot of hair, which had been pinned down atop her head, high and flat.

The cap was a boy's cap, and it matched the rest of her outfit. Amanda had shed her elaborate gown and was now dressed as a slender youth. Not only that, her masculine clothing was all in black. Had she been outside, she would have been invisible, head to toe, in the dark.

Amanda appeared to be quite at ease in her startling garb, just as though she had worn it many times before. She plopped the cap on rakishly, then approached a black leather case standing open on the table. From it, she drew, of all things, a stethoscope, which she proceeded to stuff into the inside pocket of her jacket with businesslike economy of movement. After a final quick look around the room, she picked up a pair of black leather gloves and pulled them on. Most astounding of all, she disdained the door in favor of climbing out of the second-story window. In a wink, she had pulled down the sash behind her and was gone, climbing, unburdened by suffocating corsets and twenty-five pounds of skirts and petticoats, down a convenient tree whose branches provided an easy ladder to the ground.

However unorthodox her exit, Amanda had left in the nick of time. The curtains had barely fluttered still behind her when Rutherford stomped into the lobby, shaking snow from his shoulders and banging loudly at the bell on the desk.

"Service," he thundered. "Service, please!"

Mr. Methley and his two charges had just entered the upstairs corridor outside Amanda's room when the impatient ring of the bell and Rutherford's shout reached them jarringly. Mr. Methley twitched in an automatic reflex of obedience to the summons.

"This is Miss Stone's room, number twenty," he told the girls, halting before one of the doors.

The desk bell trilled again even as the manager hovered, waiting for Sara and Felicity to deliver their life-and-death communication. Neither of them dared, in Mr. Methley's presence, to knock on Amanda's door.

"It sounds important, Mr. Methley," Sara piped up as the bell continued to jangle. She managed to fill her voice with concern for Mr. Methley's career.

Mr. Methley was torn, not wanting to leave the two girls loose on the premises and, at the same time, not wanting to ignore a paying guest needing attention—especially not a paying guest as large and demanding as Rutherford.

The paying guest won out. With a parting look that warned darkly against creating mischief, Mr. Methley turned on his heel and hurried back down the stairs towards the desk. Felicity and Sara quivered with relief.

Now Felicity's indignation returned with blazing force. "If she thinks she can come here and buy the affections of a poor boy like Gus Pike, well, a caring friend won't stand for it."

Felicity seemed to care very much indeed—perhaps as much more than a friend. She thumped smartly on the polished door, fully girded to do battle with the seductive Amanda Stone.

Sara regarded her cousin with exasperation. "You know, Felicity, you are beginning to sound more and more like Aunt Hetty."

Ignoring Sara, Felicity banged again on the door. And when there was no answer, she twisted at the door handle. It was locked tight.

Sara was disconcerted by Amanda's lack of response. She wanted Felicity and Amanda to get their shouting match over with so they could all go home.

"She has to be in there," Sara muttered. "We didn't see her leave the hotel."

Felicity pulled at the handle again, frustrated but certainly not defeated. Checking to make sure the hallway was clear, she swiftly removed a hairpin from her hair and inserted it into the keyhole while Sara stared at her in disbelief.

"What are you doing?" Sara croaked.

"Protecting Gus from that woman—and from himself."

"But we just can't break in ..."

"You'd better keep an eye out for Mr. Methley," Felicity advised coolly, jiggling the pin in the lock.

Sara scanned the corridor and her heart leapt to her throat. Bamboozling the manager was one thing, break and enter quite another.

"I don't know if this is such a good idea. I know, I'll go speak to Mr. Methley and I'll tell him that we think Miss Stone has swooned. Then he'll have to let us in, and then we could ..."

While Sara's back was turned, Felicity had conquered the lock, pushed open Amanda's door and stepped in. Before Sara could finish her sentence, she, too, was jerked inside the room, and the door was closed firmly behind her.

Downstairs at the desk, oblivious to the antics of the girls, Mr. Methley was putting on his most obliging look for the latest arrival.

"Mr. Rutherford?" he inquired.

"Yes, has the lovely young lady in room twenty returned?"

Rutherford, like Amanda before him, was making an effort, though less successfully, to keep his impatience hidden.

"Yes sir, she's retired for the night."

"I wish I could count on that," Rutherford muttered to himself.

"Beg your pardon, sir?"

Rutherford shook his head. "Nothing. I'll take my key and I'll turn in for the evening." However, the look on his face suggested that he had other plans.

Mr. Methley handed over the key with alacrity. When Rutherford headed for the stairs, the manager hurried ingratiatingly out from behind the desk.

"If you leave your boots outside the door, sir, our valet service will clean them and have them returned to you before breakfast."

Rutherford's boots could certainly have used a cleaning, what with galloping through cemeteries and kicking in lighthouse doors and so on. But he waved impatiently and disappeared up the stairway. Mr. Methley doggedly followed him, perhaps intending to wrench Rutherford's boots off himself.

In Mr. Methley's absence, Gus and Felix sped into the empty lobby. Unlike the others, they wanted nothing to do with the manager or the bell on the desk. Instead, they slipped directly up the stairs, sneaking like thieves.

"Ever since you got rich, things are a lot more exciting," Felix whispered, beginning to be pleased with their adventure, and pleased to be in out of the biting wind.

"Shhh! Be quiet, will ya, Felix?" Gus warned. If they were caught, his mission to save Amanda might be completely thwarted.

Gus and Felix had barely got to the top of the stairs when they spotted Rutherford and the manager outside Rutherford's door. Luckily, a linen closet was behind them. They barely managed to duck into it before Rutherford glanced, frowning, in their direction.

"It's no bother, Mr. Rutherford," Mr. Methley was saying, still intent upon getting possession of Rutherford's boots.

"It is to me," Rutherford shot back, beginning to look dangerously annoyed. "Good night!"

Rutherford stepped into his room and slammed the door in Mr. Methley's face. Rudely dismissed and thinking himself alone, the manager dropped his obsequious mask and allowed himself the luxury of one sizzling grimace at Rutherford's door.

As he turned back to the corridor, he suddenly remembered Sara and Felicity. They were nowhere in sight. Puzzled, he paused briefly in front of Miss Stone's door before deciding that the children must have left. With a grunt at the irritating ways of young people, he proceeded back downstairs.

Chapter Ten

Meanwhile, Amanda, the object of so much interest, had made her way to the Avonlea post office. She crouched close to the post office safe, her stethoscope pressed against it as she slowly turned the dial. Since the safe did not have any medical problems, it could only be concluded that Amanda was safecracking. Amanda, it appeared, had skills the people of Avonlea would never have imagined; she must have made up her mind to retrieve the gems herself.

The post office safe, to be honest, did not provide much of a challenge to Amanda's deft fingers. With a click, the safe released its catch, and its door swung open to reveal its secrets. But all it contained, to Amanda's immense disappointment, was a few papers and the remains of someone's lunch. She was both frustrated and impressed. Someone had been here before her.

"Rutherford, you clever snake!" she muttered, crushing the brown lunch bag in the palm of her hand.

Amanda would have been even more upset had she been able to see what was going on back at the White Sands, in her room. After Sara and

Felicity had all but tumbled inside, they pushed the door shut and stood hanging onto each other, fully expecting Amanda to spring wrathfully from behind the dressing screen. When they realized that only the flicker of the lamp burning on the table had witnessed their rude intrusion, the girls dared to look around.

The room was one of the better ones at the White Sands, furnished with shining mahogany furniture, velvet drapes and a slick horsehair sofa. The interior showed the usual signs of a female inhabitant, including clothes laid across the bed, silver-backed brushes on the dresser and, of course, the lingering scent of perfume. The leather satchel from which Amanda had taken the stethoscope stood open on a small side table. Sara approached it cautiously and peered inside, puzzled by Amanda's possession of the strange tools.

Felicity, with something else in mind, headed straight for Amanda's dressing table. And it didn't take her long to unearth what could only be, to Felicity, the tools of a wily temptress.

"English skin cream. Rouge from Paris," she listed in darkly shocked tones, paying not the slightest attention to Sara and the satchel. "French perfume ... I'll bet that without all this she's as plain as a church mouse."

Sara knew better than to argue that one with Felicity. Instead, she pulled a huge key ring from the satchel. Things had begun to hint of a good mystery.

"Look at all these keys! Suspicious, don't you think?"

"Haven't I said as much from the first we saw of her?" Felicity sputtered, in perfect, if unconscious, imitation of her Aunt Hetty.

Outside, the corridor had become silent enough for Gus and Felix to dare peep out of the linen closet. It was a good thing that peep was all they did, for, through the crack, they spotted Rutherford standing at Amanda's door, carefully turning the knob.

Sara and Felicity also heard the click. They jerked around and stared at the door, then at each other in panic.

Rutherford's eyes swept the room and found it empty—a fact that seemed to surprise him considerably. Like Felicity, he seemed to have come bent on a confrontation with his prey. He clenched his fists, frustrated.

Two steps took him to the dressing table. He pulled open the drawers and began swiftly turning over their contents, obviously searching for the jewels. Next, he dug through Amanda's luggage cases and made a rapid search behind the ornate dressing screen, still finding nothing. Finally, he flung open the doors of the huge old wardrobe that stood in the shadows against the wall.

It's a good thing the doors squeaked, or Rutherford might have caught the panicky gasp that issued from under the bed at his last action. Felicity lay flat on her stomach, squeezed like sandwich filling between the heavy bedsprings and the Turkish carpet. The gloom beneath the bed obscured her almost completely, save for the gleam of her eyes, which were wide with fright and fixed on the interior of the wardrobe through which Rutherford was rummaging.

The wardrobe was inhabited by more than dresses. When the two girls had heard Rutherford at the door, they had dived for cover. Felicity had lunged under the bed. Sara had bolted into the wardrobe, just managing to get the doors shut behind her as Rutherford stepped into the room. Now she crouched there, concealed inside one of Amanda's gowns, her head poking comically out of the decolletage. In half a second, Rutherford was going to jerk back the hanger in front of Sara and discover ...

A scraping sound from outside the window froze Rutherford in mid-search. Hastily abandoning the wardrobe, Rutherford headed for the door. Now that he'd been tearing the place apart, he apparently didn't want to get caught any more than Sara and Felicity had.

He was too late. Before he could get out, the window had been pushed up. Amanda, supple as a cat, had swung out of the tree and dropped quietly inside. As her feet touched the floor she spotted Rutherford escaping into the hallway.

"Stop right there, Robert," she called out commandingly.

And, to the utter astonishment of the hidden girls, Amanda gave chase.

As Amanda dashed after Rutherford into the corridor, Felicity squirmed from under the bed. Likewise, Sara spilled out of the wardrobe, shaking herself thankfully loose from the suffocating folds of Amanda's clothing. She was still quaking all over at so very nearly ending up in Rutherford's large, perilous hands.

Out in the hall, Amanda flew after Rutherford and grabbed him fiercely by the elbow. As he spun round, the two were so close together they were practically in each other's arms.

"I guess you think you've won," Amanda sizzled. Who else, after all, could have been to that poky little safe before her and got the jewels?

Rutherford, who towered over her, made not the slightest attempt to shake himself free. Instead, his brows flew together.

"Save your breath, Amanda. I've become impervious to your wiles."

Whatever Amanda had expected him to say, it was not this. She went quite still and searched Rutherford's face, as though she were familiar with all its moods. She found no trace of the triumph she'd expected to be there.

"You don't have the gems?" she exclaimed, startled.

Rutherford backed her up against the wall, his arm, like a bar of iron, closing her in.

"I'm never going to give up," he rumbled. "And you can't escape. No matter where you go, every time you turn around, I'll be there, watching. You made a big mistake when you took on Robert Rutherford."

Rutherford's lids were half lowered and his head bent over the slim figure backed against the flocked wallpaper. In fact, anyone stumbling unsuspecting upon the scene might have sworn it was some lover's quarrel—especially from the way Amanda was looking back at Rutherford. Her cheeks flamed with color and her eyes began to sparkle, almost as though she thoroughly enjoyed sparring with the man. Almost as though she gloried in his hot pursuit ...

Whatever she might have done next was prevented by a clatter of boots as Gus and Felix burst from the linen closet. Gus had no intention of allowing Amanda to be imprisoned in the arms of that detestable man.

"Go and get Methley!" Gus ordered Felix, never taking his eye from Rutherford. If there ever was a time for a rescuer to rush in, Gus thought, it certainly was now. "Leave her be!" he shouted.

Gus didn't wait to be hit. Without a single thought to the consequences, he put his head down and galloped straight at Rutherford, striking the big man soundly in the solar plexus. The force of the impact caused Rutherford to stagger back and double over as the breath was knocked out of him. Amanda, who never stayed around for violent scenes, took the opportunity to flee towards her room—only to run smack into Sara and Felicity. Gasping, Rutherford still managed to lurch after her and grasp Amanda's arm, preventing her complete getaway.

"I said leave her be or I'll have at you again!" Gus roared, gathering himself for another charge.

Still clutching his struggling captive, Rutherford reached into his coat and pulled out a leather wallet. Felix arrived at the very same moment, with an agitated Mr. Methley at his heels.

"What's going on here?" Methley demanded, outraged by the presence of the troublesome children and appalled at an attack upon one of his well-bred guests. And when he recognized Amanda, dressed in male clothing, his eyes fairly popped from his head.

"Amanda Stone," Rutherford panted, "I hereby arrest you for the theft of the Van Dusen jewels."

"You can't arrest no one," Gus intervened.

"Oh no, boy?" Rutherford, with obvious relish, brandished a large metal badge in all their faces. "I'm with the McGrath Detective Agency of Boston, hired by the family. And what's more, you, boy," he fixed Gus with a particularly vindictive glare, "you are under arrest for aiding and abetting, receiving stolen goods and interfering with an officer of the law in the pursuit of his duty."

Everyone gaped in dismay at Gus. Gus stared in turn at Amanda. Trapped for the moment, Amanda at least had the presence of mind to shrink demurely and let a big, sad tear roll down her cheek.

Chapter Eleven

The wheels of the law swung creakily into motion, with uncomfortable consequences to those involved. In the dark of night, Felix and Gus found themselves conveyed to the Markdale Jail, and the next morning dawned with the pair sharing a dank little cell in the building's depths.

As might well be expected, Gus stood slumped against the bars looking somber and depressed. Felix, on the other hand, was having the time of his life. Now that he was warm and dry and had been fed a substantial breakfast, he could look back upon his night's adventure from the perspective of a principal player. Not only had he got to witness secret meetings in a cemetery, he had been in on the capture of a lady jewel thief dressed for one of her forays, and he had managed to get himself arrested right alongside Gus.

From the stout iron bars on the window to the rough gray blanket over the hard bunk—it was almost all too thrilling for a fellow to take in! Felix found it exhilarating to be an actual prisoner, despite the obvious inadequacies of the cell. So exhilarating that he managed to swallow his disappointment over the fact that they were housed above ground and not in a dark crypt, and that the

Markdale Jail proved lamentably short of chains, groans, starving rats and instruments of torture.

Lord Doom certainly would have done a better job of imprisonment than the Markdale constable, Felix knew. To pass the time, he had begun recounting the plot of the magazine serial to Gus. Gus was too distracted to object and was, besides, a captive audience.

"So then the bad guy ..."

"Lord Doom," Gus furnished. He had learned, in the intervening hours, a great deal more than he ever wanted to know about deranged European aristocrats.

Felix nodded enthusiastically, wishing their cell had a few spiders or, at the very least, a message scratched into a wall by some despairing previous prisoner.

"... goes out for these horse rides when it's a full moon all dressed in black, killing people on account of a broken heart. Oh, I know it sounds stupid but that's the story, Gus."

Gus didn't reply, even to comment upon Rutherford. While he didn't hold with galloping about the countryside committing mayhem, he was beginning to suspect the desperate lengths a fellow could be driven to on account of his heart.

"Gus, are you listening?"

"Yeah," mumbled Gus despondently, wishing he were anywhere else but in the Markdale lockup.

Felix settled himself more comfortably against the wall, not noticing how distracted his audience was.

"Meanwhile, the good guy, Sir Basil Oxenford," he continued with gusto, "is digging a hole figuring Lord Doom will walk along, fall in and be captured."

Gus was saved from more by the voice of Hetty King, echoing in the anteroom.

"Hurry up now, Constable," she was saying impatiently. "I am most disappointed ... utterly ludicrous example of shoddy, irresponsible police work, really, Constable."

"Aunt Hetty's come to save us," Felix groaned. He didn't relish being released into Hetty's businesslike hands.

Hetty and the beleaguered Markdale constable appeared outside the cell.

Felix jumped up. "Look, Aunt Hetty, I'm arrested," he announced, as though he had just won the provincial spelling bee.

Hetty glared accusingly at the constable. Never, within living memory, had a member of the King family been put in jail.

"Get them out of there this instant!"

The constable stood his ground bravely. "Miss King, they're arrested. Gus Pike is an accomplice to a world-famous jewel thief and Mr. Methley is charging young Felix here with trespassing."

By way of answer, Hetty slapped an envelope into the constable's hand. "Mr. Methley has seen fit to change his mind after a brief chat with me. Here, read this. As for Gus Pike, it's obvious he had no idea those gems were stolen when he accepted them. Clearly, that Amanda Stone took advantage of his helpful nature."

That was very accurately put. Unfortunately, Gus didn't believe it. He sprang upright.

"That's not true ..."

"Quiet now, Gus," Hetty warned. "I'm trying to help you."

"I'll never believe Miss Stone to be a criminal," Gus announced impetuously. "She's been wronged."

The constable, considering himself much wiser in the ways of the world, shook his head at Gus's folly. He had not had to deal directly with the potent charms of the lady in question. "The man from the McGrath Detective Agency says you're not the first young lad who's had his head turned by Amanda Stone."

Hetty pounced on the statement, taking the

offensive immediately. "Oh well, I am sure that the attorney general will be most interested to know that his constabulary is now taking direction from the McGrath Agency of Boston."

The constable weakened a little but still clung to his position. "The fact is," he pointed out, "those jewels were unaccounted for. They were not in Miss Stone's room and they were not in the post office safe this morning."

This statement gave Hetty occasion for positively gleeful triumph. "Well, a proper policeman might have considered asking the postmistress a question or two, and so would have discovered that I have the jewels. Here."

She produced the bag of gems from her handbag and waved them in the air, savoring the constable's astonishment.

"I tried to return them to Gus last night, in fact, but he was not home, you see."

"Miss King, those jewels are the rightful property of Miss Stone, I know that," Gus protested, apparently determined to ruin the case for his own release.

"Oh don't be absurd, boy," Hetty rasped in exasperation. "Hurry up now, Constable."

She thrust the bag of jewels at the constable, who sighed, produced his key ring and capitulated.

Hetty turned her attention to the miscreants in the cell. "I am most disappointed with you boys. Wandering heaven knows where at all hours of the night, consorting with ruffians, cavorting around hotels, going to jail of all things! March!"

As they came out of the cell, Hetty seemed barely able to restrain herself from grabbing their ears and frog-marching them ahead of her.

Felix was heartbroken at his easy deliverance. "Just when I was getting to feel like a real criminal," he lamented, casting a look fondly back into the cell.

"Good day to you," Hetty tossed at the defeated constable as she hustled her charges from sight.

Chapter Twelve

The day after the boys had been sprung from prison, they walked with Sara and Felicity towards the lighthouse, talking the matter over.

Felicity bristled with indignation. "It's written all over her face—Amanda Stone's soul is black with crime."

"Sara even saw her burglar tools," Felix added, wishing mightily he could have got a look into the satchel himself.

Gus was still cherishing his exalted image of that larcenous lady, and he glanced sharply at Sara for confirmation of this damning fact. Sara nodded reluctantly, causing Gus to sigh a heavy sigh. One could almost hear his illusions breaking to pieces around him.

"Gus, why don't you come and join us for dinner?" Sara invited, hoping that a little cheerful company might console her friend.

Gus only kicked at the dirt. "I just feel like being alone for now."

At this evidence that Gus was still affected by Amanda, Felicity began to swell up. Gus, it seemed, just had no common sense.

"I've never heard of anything so ridiculous!" she sputtered. "You're going to moon over this strange woman when your friends are—?"

Fortunately, Sara jerked Felicity by the elbow and managed to shush her before Gus got a complete tongue-lashing.

The children halted at the turnoff to the farm and stood watching as Gus trudged on up to the lighthouse, presumably to brood over his troubles. After the door shut behind him, they turned to go home. There was still the matter of getting themselves something to eat.

As for Gus, he might have intended to brood,

but when he stepped into his home, all such ideas were driven from his head by the sight that confronted him. A whirlwind might very well have just torn through the place for the mess the interior of the lighthouse was in. Clothes and fishing tackle and pots lay strewn about. What's more, the heavy trunk covering Captain Crane's secret hiding place had been pulled aside.

Worst of all, a familiar and very unsailorlike fragrance lingered in the air. Gus pulled Amanda's handkerchief from his bosom, where he had been guarding it, and sniffed in its scent, very perplexed. Oh yes, it was the very same that hovered in the room.

Just as Gus was coming to some rather uncomfortable conclusions, a hand snaked out from behind and grasped him by the throat. The other flashed a knife before Gus's face. Naturally, it was Rutherford.

"You see that, boy?" Rutherford growled, positively radiating menace. "Nothing quite like honed steel, is there?"

"What do you want?" Gus was choking under the arm clamped round his neck.

"I have Amanda," Rutherford told him. "If you do not bring me the gems I will kill her. I'll bring the body back here and I'll make it seem as though you did it, and, by God, I guarantee that you will hang. Amanda for the gems. Tonight, at the old cemetery, after dark. Do you understand?"

Teeth clenched, Gus could only nod. Grunting his satisfaction, Rutherford flung Gus to the floor and strode out.

It didn't take Gus long to reach the King farmhouse. This time, he was going to take the precaution of consulting with his friends before getting into any more trouble. Sitting with Felix, Sara and Felicity at the kitchen table, he described the new twist the story had taken.

"He said that if I didn't give him the gems tonight, he'd kill Amanda," Gus finished up, delivering the final shocker.

The children exchanged looks, growing pale. This wasn't the sort of problem people were used to in Avonlea.

"I don't think the police are supposed to do that, are they? Even detectives." Felix frowned. His grip on the law might have been hazy, but he was certain it didn't extend to using threats of murder. Certainly the placid local constable would have fainted away at the very idea of using the tactics Rutherford was resorting to.

"Then he said he'd make it look like I did it,"

Gus added miserably, somehow never doubting Rutherford's ability to do so.

"Do you think Amanda's innocent?" Sara asked, her brow wrinkled with the problem.

"I don't think so," asserted Felicity stoutly. "We should tell Aunt Hetty."

Though the time certainly seemed right to start consulting adults, Gus shook his head vigorously. He could imagine only too well what Hetty King would do with such a situation. And if Hetty had just handed over the gems when Gus had asked for them, none of this would be happening now.

"No, I can't do that now. It's too complicated. And dangerous. I have to help Amanda myself. I can't let Rutherford hurt her."

With Amanda's life at stake, Gus couldn't take the risk of anything going wrong. Slowly, he began to twist a ring from his finger. It was a heavy gold ring containing a valuable ruby, the only possession Gus had of any consequence. It had been Captain Crane's parting gift as a reward for Gus's help in retrieving the captain's own valuables.

"Gus, you can't give him that!" Sara cried, appalled. She knew how very proud Gus was of that ring, and how deeply attached he was to it.

Gus shook his head. "It's all I have. It'll have to be enough."

"I know," exclaimed Felix suddenly, "we can use mother's jewelry to save Amanda."

"Felix ..." Felicity reproved. The boy obviously had no idea of the difference between a farm wife's costume jewelry and the fortune the real gems represented.

Felicity was about to dismiss her brother's crazy idea—then she sat up very straight in her chair. If the transaction took place in the dark, and no one got a close look at what was being handed over, perhaps Rutherford really could be fooled by fakes!

Felicity's gaze flew to the rhinestones she had been sewing on her dress. They were exceptionally big ones, brilliantly colored. Excitement gripped her. "What about these?" she suggested, snatching up a handful.

The lamplight caught the baubles in Felicity's palm, causing them to glitter like rare Arabian delights. To the unsophisticated eyes around the table, the rhinestones easily passed for stones of fabulous worth.

Gus jammed his own ruby ring back onto his finger and looked as though a one-ton weight had just been lifted from his shoulders. He was so relieved he jumped to his feet and picked Felicity up and twirled her clear off the ground.

"That's just the ticket, Felicity," he exulted.

Before he knew what he was doing, he had given Felicity an enormous hug.

Felicity was so surprised she couldn't say a word. Her cheeks flamed pink and her mouth flapped open. And when Gus released her, she had to struggle to regain her composure before the curious eyes of her cousins. As for Gus, he headed out the door as fast as he could go, not leaving so much as a hint about his plans.

"Now you're getting into the spirit of things, Felicity." Felix approved. Now that the prospect of bloody murder seemed to have been averted, he was starting to recover his sense of adventure.

Just down the lane in Rose Cottage, Hetty King, all unsuspecting, considered the local drama closed. After checking to make sure she was safely alone, she had slipped the magazine from its hiding place and opened it to the infamously lurid serial that had so enthralled the children. She sat curled up in her corner, snug and cozy, while lightning flashed outside. She cracked nuts as she read, devouring them one after the other as she became more and more engrossed in the story. By the time Olivia sped in from the storm, Hetty was so carried away that she didn't even hear the door slam behind her sister.

As Olivia pulled off her gloves, she was highly amused to see what Hetty was reading. Chuckling to herself, she tiptoed up behind Hetty.

"What's happening?" Olivia asked in a low, smooth voice.

Hetty didn't even lift her eyes. "Lord Doom has set a price of a thousand pounds on poor Sir Basil's head," she murmured, turning a page avidly.

Olivia grinned even wider. "Is that in the recipe section?"

Realizing at last that someone else was in the room, Hetty's head jerked up.

"Olivia!" she squawked, as though her sister had deliberately materialized from thin air in order to catch her reading trash. "Why, I'm reading this rubbish merely as ammunition in order to write a letter of protest to the editor, you see. Nut?" she offered, to fend off Olivia's knowing and totally skeptical look.

Hetty would have dropped Lord Doom like a hot coal had she known that, at that very moment, Sara and Felicity were slogging through the cold towards the lighthouse to play out their promised part in Gus's drama.

"Mother's going to kill me," Felicity lamented.

Sara agreed, equally glum. "I've noticed that

every time we try to help someone, we end up in trouble."

In the lighthouse, Gus lay sprawled on his bed, obviously exhausted and covered with grime. He didn't even move at the sound of a knock.

"Gus," Felicity called. She was worried and wanted in from the wind.

"Who's there?"

"Felicity King and Sara Stanley."

At once, Gus jumped up and flung the door open for his visitors.

"Do you have them?" he wanted to know, before the two were even fully inside.

Felicity reached into her pocket and produced a small bag, lumpy with the rhinestones. She had sewn the bag specially to resemble the sack the real gems were in.

"Do you really think this is going to work?" Sara asked, very worried about the venture.

Gus nodded, trying to radiate confidence. "It could be days before Rutherford finds out they're not the real gems."

He reached for the precious bag, but Felicity pulled it back. She wasn't giving up her advantage without a fight.

"You shouldn't do this alone, Gus. You need friends to help you."

"Too dangerous ..."

"And what if she asks you to go with her?" Felicity demanded, finally giving voice to her worst fear.

"What?"

"She won't stay in Avonlea. She'll want to leave. Maybe she'll want you to go with her. Will you?"

In the face of Felicity's wide-eyed look, Gus could only shrug. "I don't know," he confessed.

Felicity winced at his answer, and Gus saw. He reached out for the jewel bag again but clasped Felicity's hands in his own instead.

"Would it matter to you?" he asked quietly.

Felicity struggled with conflicting desires—one to spill her feelings to Gus, the other to retain her dignity. Dignity won. She snatched her fingers away, leaving Gus with the rhinestones.

"Not in the least, Gus Pike," Felicity rapped out, her nose in the air. "What you do with your life is your own business. But I'll tell you one thing, as a friend who has some concern for your well-being, that Amanda Stone is nothing but trouble from head to toe."

Gus already knew that little fact for himself. He watched, overwhelmed and bewildered, as Felicity turned on her heel and marched out of the lighthouse, slamming the door behind her. He looked to Sara for help, only to find Sara thoroughly annoyed with the both of them.

"You two ..." she muttered, and she stomped out as well.

Outside, Sara and Felicity marched along in strained silence. Felicity walked so fast that Sara had to trot to keep up.

"Felicity, this is not a footrace!"

Irked, Felicity came to a halt, hands on hips.

"If you like him, why don't you just tell him," Sara shot out, annoyed herself. The strain of trying to help foil a murder while her friends quarreled would tell on anybody.

"If I like who?"

"Gus."

"Don't be ridiculous," Felicity snapped, starting hotly down the path again.

Sara started after her.

"Well, he likes you."

This brought Felicity to a halt again.

"Really?"

Stars appeared briefly in Felicity's eyes. Then she remembered herself. Her chin twitched up. "I intend to set my sights higher than a dirt-covered boy who lives in an old lighthouse."

"Felicity King! What a terrible thing to say,"

Sara cried, genuinely shocked. "You can't possibly mean that."

Felicity didn't, but she certainly wasn't going to tell Sara.

"I'll thank you to mind your own business," she said. "You think you are the big authority on romance in Avonlea. Well, you don't know everything."

"I know what I see," Sara fired back.

Further argument was of no use. A great crash of thunder made both girls jump. Felicity set off again, almost at a run, with Sara doing her best to keep up.

Chapter Thirteen

Adventures with jewel thieves or not, Sara's instruction in domestic arts at the King farmhouse continued. While the other children did their own chores, Sara was left once again to prepare the supper. The art of cooking remained as mysterious and impenetrable to her as it had on previous occasions. When the children finally gathered around the table, Sara served up the results of her labors—small round objects that closely resembled lumps of coal.

Felix, Cecily and Felicity all scowled in disappointment, for their work had made them ravenous. While a flash of lightning illuminated the room, Felix tried to take a bite from the mystery food.

"What's this? Charcoal?" he groused, listening to the thing drop back on his plate with a clunk.

Part of the reason the food was so bad was that Sara's mind had not been on cooking at all, but on Gus's dilemma. She scarcely heard Felix.

"If only we knew the plan ..." she agonized, the pot and serving spoon forgotten in her hands. There was no telling what sort of trouble Gus might get himself into trying to cope with Rutherford by himself.

Felicity, too, had been so wrapped up in Gus's problems that she didn't have a comment to spare for the culinary disaster before her.

"We know enough, I think," she put in bleakly.

She and Sara exchanged looks. Without saying a word, they both knew they couldn't leave Gus out there on his own with that terrible man.

"We'll take Digger," Felicity said, rising to her feet.

"Yes. He hates that detective."

Sara readily abandoned the pot on the back of the stove while Felicity turned to her younger sister.

"Cecily ..."

"I know ... stay here," Cecily sighed. Whatever exciting adventures the others were going on, she was never allowed to join.

"If we're not back by midnight," Sara instructed, "you go and get help. Come on, Felix! Hurry!"

"I haven't finished eating my ..." Felix looked at the charred lump and thought the better of wolfing down such a dinner. "All right, let's go."

As fast as they could, the three children pulled on their coats and raced to the cemetery. Once there, they cautiously scanned the scene under cover of the bushes. The only person they could see was Gus himself, pacing back and forth by the light of a lantern, which he had hung from the branch of a tree.

The lantern cast a very puny glow in the blackness all around, for no scrap of moonlight could make its way from behind the dense storm clouds. The branches creaked and groaned in the erratic gusts of wind. An owl hooted ominously. Lightning threw an eerie light onto the gravestones. In such a setting, it was no wonder that Gus appeared to be shivering.

"He looks cold," Felicity murmured, worried that Gus might catch pneumonia in that inadequate jacket of his.

The children hid themselves behind some tombstones in order to keep watch. This time, Felix was holding Digger tightly so that the eager dog would not give them away. All of them went rigid when a flare of lightning suddenly revealed the silhouette of Rutherford not a dozen yards away.

"Have you got what I want, boy?" Rutherford called out to Gus.

Gus spun around at the sound of the hated voice. "Where's Miss Stone?" he demanded, getting straight to his main concern. He was determined Rutherford should keep his part of the bargain.

"I'm all right, Gus," came Amanda's voice over the gusting wind. It was so dark, nobody could see her.

"Throw the gems this way, boy," Rutherford ordered.

"Not until I see Miss Stone."

Rutherford dragged Amanda, wrists bound, into view and pushed her ahead of him until the lantern light illuminated her cloak.

"Here she is," Rutherford growled impatiently. "Where's my property?"

"Miss Stone, are you all right?" Gus asked, unable to take his distressed gaze from her captive state.

Amanda ran quickly to Gus and placed her bound arms around his neck as though he had saved her from certain death. Her seduction had never been more powerful.

"Oh, do as he says, Gus," she pleaded fetchingly. "He's a monster!"

As if to prove her words, Rutherford loomed up behind her.

"Throw the gems here, boy, or by God I'll bash you against these stones!"

Gus hesitated a long moment before finally pulling the little cloth bag from his jacket and tossing it over to Rutherford. Rutherford caught it eagerly, jerked open the neck and poured the contents into his palm. As best he could, he examined them by the wind-buffeted lantern light.

"Well, Robert?" Amanda inquired, with much more pleasantness towards her captor than might have been expected from a woman in her position.

All the children held their breaths, for the bag contained nothing but Felicity's rhinestones. If Rutherford noticed the deception there was no telling what he might do.

The rhinestones did glitter convincingly. Rutherford hesitated, then poured his shining handful triumphantly back into the bag. The weak lantern light had done its job.

"Yes ... this is it!"

"I told you it had to be the boy," Amanda said companionably to Rutherford. "Who else could it be?" She turned to Gus. "There's a good lad!" she told him, as though he were a pet who had finally performed as expected.

She let go of Gus and unbound her own hands easily—a very odd thing for a captive under threat of death.

From behind the gravestones, Felix, Felicity and Sara looked at each other in amazement.

"Miss Stone, what's going on?" Gus demanded, much confused by her easy freedom and beginning to arrive at some very unwelcome conclusions.

"I knew it," Felicity hissed in high indignation from her hiding place. "I tried to tell everyone but no one listened to me."

Gus moved a little farther away from the lantern. Rutherford stuffed the bag of fake gems into his pocket and jerked his head at his captive.

"Let's go, Amanda."

Rutherford spoke as though it were perfectly natural that a woman would want to trot away with the very man who had threatened to murder her moments before. And, what's more, Amanda seemed perfectly willing to listen. In fact, she looked quite smugly pleased with herself.

A small croaking sound from Gus made her stop. She turned back to him, perhaps in recognition of all the trouble Gus had gone to on her behalf.

"Mr. Rutherford and I were partners," she explained softly to the dismayed boy. "We had a falling out, harsh words were spoken ..."

"Yes," put in Rutherford, eyeing Amanda's graceful figure, "it was a double-cross, which she now regrets, don't you, my sweet?"

"Yes, of course, Robert," Amanda trilled. Then she bent over confidentially towards Gus. "He's as tenacious as a bloodhound. I suspect he's in love with me," she whispered, sounding mightily pleased with the situation.

Rutherford's term of endearment and Amanda's cheerful answer seemed to have some final, catastrophic effect on Gus. He quite unexpectedly grabbed Amanda by the arm.

"Ouch! Let go! Oh!" Amanda yelped, struggling.

Her cry caused Rutherford to swing around and take a few menacing steps towards Gus. Gus moved away, still holding onto Amanda and pulling her with him.

"Let her go, boy," Rutherford said threateningly, advancing more quickly.

"He'll hurt you," warned Amanda melodramatically. "I won't be able to stop him." She seemed torn between seriously trying to save Gus and being pleased with Rutherford's passion.

Rutherford took a large, angry step towards Gus, raising his stick. "By God, I'm sick and tired of you. I'm going to thrash your ..."

Before the cane could lash down on Gus, a chestnut zinged out of the darkness, striking Rutherford a stinging blow on the face. Another followed, then another, whacking Rutherford hard in every part of his anatomy. Felix, Felicity and Sara leapt out of their hiding place, throwing the missiles with all their might.

In the emergency, all they could find to throw were chestnuts and snowballs, but they made the most of them, especially since the chestnuts were still inside their thick, spiky green jackets. Digger, also released, sprang, barking furiously, at the man he detested so much. Despite these assaults, Rutherford kept on after Gus, meaning to slash him if he could.

The last step Rutherford took brought him up short, for he suddenly found himself teetering on the edge of a deep, dark, completely unsuspected pit. As he tried to scramble back, one of Felix's deadly-true missiles struck him with a great thud right between the eyes. Unable to stop himself, Rutherford toppled, face forward, straight into the hole.

The second Rutherford struck the bottom, Gus let go of Amanda and rushed over to the pit to look in. Rutherford lay sprawled, apparently knocked out cold. And, for good measure, he was also tangled up in the fishnet that had dropped around him. He had lost the jewel bag as he fell. Rhinestones winked up, scattered every which way in the mud.

Amanda's mouth popped open with the realization that she had just been used as bait to lure Rutherford to the hole. In the barest nick of time she prevented herself from screeching in protest.

Sara and her cousins rushed up a moment later. When Sara saw the trap Gus had laid, she recognized it immediately.

"Just like the one Sir Basil used to catch evil Lord Doom in 'Death Rides by Night'!" she cried out in admiration.

"Hey," put in Felix, "I told Gus about that!" And here he'd been thinking that Gus hadn't been listening at all back there in the Markdale Jail.

Gus grinned. "Took me all afternoon to dig that hole and get the muck out. My back's near broke."

Amanda was a woman accustomed to thinking on her feet. She hurried to Gus's side and gazed up at him in hero worship.

"I owe you a great debt, once again, Gus. He

took me captive and he told me he was going to kill you! I couldn't bear the thought of that so—"

"Was he holding you captive when you helped him tear apart my home today?" Gus interrupted, strangely unmoved by Amanda's appealing eyes.

Missing Gus's tone, Amanda pressed a dainty hand to her bosom. "Oh, he took me there by force!" she quavered.

"And who was it who told him about the Captain's secret hiding place?"

Amanda saw that her hold over Gus was definitely slipping. Determined to overwhelm him with an all-out barrage of her charms, she reached up and stroked Gus's cheek. Then she brought her soft lips close to his and gazed seductively into his eyes. Gus bent closer—and gave Amanda a little tip backward. With a screech, she fell smack into the pit with Rutherford. Felicity, Sara and Felix giggled with delight.

"I wasn't about to believe her again," Gus admitted. "That'd make me stupid."

Felicity and Gus smiled openly at each other, friendship restored.

"I guess I owe you all an apology," Gus continued. "Especially you, Felicity. You knew from the beginning."

Felicity's head lifted proudly. "Everyone

knows I'm a shrewd judge of character, Gus. I was telling Sara that, despite your lack of prospects, your inner strength would see you through, didn't I, Sara?"

"Uh ... yes, Felicity." Sara just stopped herself from blurting out that Felicity had said no such thing.

"And I want you all to know I appreciate it," Gus said. "I'll never again lose sight of my true friends just because of a pretty face."

Amanda, thanks to landing squarely on top of Rutherford, hadn't been harmed in the least. As soon as she hit bottom, she sprang up again, ignoring Rutherford completely in favor of the scattered gems. As fast as she could she began scooping them up from the corners of the pit where they had rolled. In doing so, she got a closer look at them.

"Hey," came her outraged voice as Rutherford stirred groggily, "these aren't the real gems. Where are they, you bloody fool?"

She hadn't been a successful jewel thief for years without becoming an expert on quality. Even in the feeble gleams of lantern light that penetrated the hole, she knew Rutherford had been tricked.

"Safe in the Markdale constable's safe," Felix

gloated before he could think about what he was so foolishly giving away."

Rutherford had regained consciousness and Amanda's words seemed to have a totally electric effect upon him. Tearing the fishnet from himself as though it were mere cobwebs, he suddenly sprang to his feet inside the pit. He was fuming mad and looked bent on murder.

"Gus! Look out!" Felix yelled as the dark apparition rose up from the dark hole. With a bare split second to spare, Felix grabbed at Gus, pulling him just short of Rutherford's enraged grasp.

Gus had miscalculated Rutherford's size and failed to dig the pit deep enough. Now, before Gus's horrified eyes, Rutherford clambered out of it, smeared with mud and frightening enough to be Lord Doom himself. The children backed away, barely able to move, as Rutherford heaved himself to his feet and lunged towards them. Lightning illuminated the contorted fury of his face.

"Robert!" shrieked Amanda from the depths of the pit. "Robert! Robert!"

Her voice broke the spell of terror, enabling all the young people, including Gus, to regain full use of their legs. Leaping tombstones and crashing through brush, they fled as fast as their fright would carry them, Gus towing Felicity along by the arm. Rutherford made to pursue them and had actually started off when Amanda called out again.

"Robert—aren't you forgetting something?"

Rutherford paused, sneering back towards the hole where Amanda was so neatly captured.

"Give me one good reason why I should bother with you," he insisted angrily.

Even trapped in a muddy pit in a cemetery, Amanda's wits did not desert her. "The Markdale constable's safe. Should be an easy job—for the two of us."

Rutherford paused a moment longer, then reached down and hauled Amanda out of the hole. She clung to him for a moment, turning on him the same alluring gaze she had used on Gus, then broke away. With the air of a man who should know better but can't help himself, Rutherford started to follow her. A moment later, the two flitted off out of sight together.

Chapter Fourteen

As soon as the fleeing children realized that Rutherford wasn't pounding after them, they stumbled to a halt at the edge of a poplar stand and stood bent over, gasping for breath. When they managed to gather their wits, all eyes focused accusingly on Felix. He was the one who had blabbed about the real jewels being in the Markdale safe. It seemed obvious where Rutherford and Amanda would head.

"We have to go there," Sara asserted urgently. "We have to warn the constable."

The idea was a noble one, but by the time they got there they were too late. The Markdale constable had found out for himself the perils of having a pair such as Rutherford and Amanda loose in the neighborhood. The children discovered him nursing a large lump on his head and mournfully contemplating the empty interior of his safe.

"I woke up and the gems were gone," he lamented as Felicity and Sara hurriedly applied a makeshift ice-pack to his head.

Gus grimaced, realizing that he himself bore a lot of the blame for the way things had turned out. "I should have told the truth about those gems in the first place," he groaned.

Felicity gingerly patted the ice at the constable's hairline, then turned to the others. Once again, she remembered that she was supposed to be in charge of the King household.

"Well, I'll tell you one thing, if Mother and

Father ever find out, they'll never leave Avonlea again."

After the constable was on his feet and the small office tidied up, there seemed to be nothing more for the young people to do but go home again and swear to stay clear of any more bamboozling strangers. At a time when all ordinary children ought to have been in their beds, the little party, Gus included, retired to the farmhouse kitchen to further contemplate their escapades.

Adventuring, as Felix long ago could have told them, turned out be a hungry business. Sara had provided nothing edible for their supper, and with all the running about the countryside in fear of their lives they had worked up a gigantic appetite. Felicity applied herself to the problem and soon the kitchen table was piled with everything edible that was left in the house. Cheese, bread, butter, jam, biscuits, raisins, dried fruit and more were sacrificed to refuel the party.

"I suppose they'll be far away by now," Sara said with a resigned sigh. In hindsight, she couldn't believe that she and Felicity had actually broken into Amanda's hotel room. She quaked in her shoes to think what her Aunt Hetty would have done had she and Felicity been arrested for trespassing too.

"And good riddance to them," Felix asserted,

stuffing his mouth with a huge date square. He had had more than enough of the whole business.

"Sorry I got you into this mess," Gus said sheepishly.

"I'm just sorry that Miss Stone escaped punishment," said Felicity, just as though she would have been quite happy to have seen Amanda led away in chains.

"Well," Sara told her confidently, despite the Markdale officer's condition, "the constable will be after them now."

No one commented that, considering the episode of the safe, the Markdale constable wasn't likely to be much of a threat to the two resourceful fugitives.

"But what I want to know," Felix put in, "is what happened to Lord Doom after *he* fell into the pit?"

All the children brightened at the thought of at least one trap working as it ought. Gus picked up the magazine from the kitchen table, where they had left it before going out. Proudly, he demonstrated his new reading skills.

"'When the villagers looked down at the Count's crumpled body,'" he began, "'his black clothing stained by scarlet blood in the torchlight, they could see the fire in his eyes was not dampened. And that fire was the fire of madness; the fire that had sent him out in the night on his bloody rampages, to ride his black horse in search of victims was jealousy for the love of a pure maiden he could not obtain.'"

The children grew so engrossed that they all jumped in their chairs as Digger suddenly barked and rushed to the door. Gus, nearest to the door, opened it obligingly, and Digger bolted outside.

"Oh, no!" Felicity squealed, realizing that Gus didn't know how Digger had led them into the adventure in the first place.

"Not again!" Felix echoed.

The children jumped up to get their coats and pursue their dog.

Digger, it seemed, couldn't leave well enough alone either. He headed towards the cliffs, barking excitedly. And he had good reason to bark, for a horse hurtled along, at full gallop, hot breath steaming from its nostrils.

While the children had been dashing to Markdale and back, the threatening storm clouds had rolled away, leaving a clear sky and a full, bright moon. The children, running after the dog, were silhouetted in the moonlight. Then another silhouette appeared, showing up sharply against the moon-sparkling sea.

It was, of course, Amanda, her hood thrown

back, her hair streaming behind her. She looked over her shoulder as she ran and she clutched in her hand the oh-so-familiar bag of gems. In the distance, a dog howled.

Far behind, Rutherford, caped and ominous, whipped his black horse for more speed. He called out into the wind.

"You'll never escape, Amanda Stone. I'll chase you to the ends of the earth!"

Rutherford's words echoed back to the children, who stood and watched as the villain caught Amanda and lifted her onto the saddle in front of him. And they could have sworn Amanda was laughing, confident that she could outwit Rutherford, or anyone else who got in her way. This time, they had the sense to realize just how much Amanda enjoyed the game. And they were quite content to allow the pair, gems and all, to dash out of sight. Let them cause trouble somewhere else and leave the people of Avonlea to their peaceful, uneventful lives.

❦   ❦   ❦